"I trust you."

That was what he wanted, right? Her complete faith in him so she wouldn't question any command required to keep her safe.

Jason tilted his head to the cave's damp black ceiling, taking a moment to get his head back in the survival game before he blew this mission, too. "All right, then. Let's move out before Buck and his men rappel down the cliff and figure out which of these passages cuts through to the other side of the gorge."

"You know, though, right?" She waved off that moment of doubt. "I said I trust you, and I do. How many rules are we up to now? Six or seven? Keep moving? Step where you step? I've got them memorized now."

"Don't let go of my hand." He couldn't risk her getting turned around and wandering away down the wrong passage.

"No problem with that," she assured him, latching on with both hands. "Lead on."

As Sam willingly followed him into the darkness, he wondered if her ready trust in him would be an even more dangerous mistake than that kiss.

RESCUED BY THE MARINE

USA TODAY Bestselling Author

JULIE MILLER

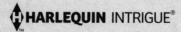

HARLEQUIN INTRIGUE®

For my father-in-law, Howard Miller, and his lady, Dotty Robarge.

A Navy veteran and the widow of an Air Force veteran.
Now a fun, lovely couple.

Thank you both for your service to our country.

ISBN-13: 978-1-335-52667-0

Recycling programs
for this product may
not exist in your area.

Rescued by the Marine

Copyright © 2018 by Julie Miller

Printed in U.S.A.

Julie Miller is an award-winning *USA TODAY* bestselling author of breathtaking romantic suspense—with a National Readers' Choice Award and a Daphne du Maurier Award, among other prizes. She has also earned an *RT Book Reviews* Career Achievement Award. For a complete list of her books, monthly newsletter and more, go to juliemiller.org.

Books by Julie Miller

Harlequin Intrigue

Rescued by the Marine

The Precinct

Beauty and the Badge
Takedown
KCPD Protector
Crossfire Christmas
Military Grade Mistletoe
Kansas City Cop

The Precinct: Bachelors in Blue

APB: Baby
Kansas City Countdown
Necessary Action
Protection Detail

The Precinct: Cold Case

Kansas City Cover-Up
Kansas City Secrets
Kansas City Confessions

Visit the Author Profile page at Harlequin.com.

CAST OF CHARACTERS

Jason Hunt—They don't come any tougher than this veteran Marine turned mountain man and search-and-rescue expert. After all he's lost, Jason needs the solitude of the Wyoming wilderness to deal with his post-traumatic stress. Will answering the call to save a kidnapped heiress bring him redemption and healing? Or will this mission cost him what little heart and soul he has left?

Samantha Eddington—History repeats itself when this nerdy, nearsighted heiress is abducted on the anniversary of her mother's kidnapping and murder. Survival means more than staying one step ahead of the mercenaries who are willing to trade her life for her father's fortune. She must also learn the rules of the mountain...and unlock the secrets of her brawny, taciturn rescuer.

Walter Eddington—Founder of the Midas Group, a billion-dollar hotel and resort empire. Samantha's father has already survived one tragedy. With his failing health, he won't survive another.

Joyce Eddington—Samantha's stepmother will do whatever is necessary to protect her husband and his business empire.

Taylor Eddington—Samantha's stepsister. Younger, prettier and far more suited to the social demands of being an Eddington than Samantha will ever be.

Kyle Grazer—Samantha's ex-boyfriend thinks a proposal will make up for his cheating.

Dante Pellegrino—The director of security for the Midas Group.

Brandon Metz—Samantha's personal bodyguard.

Richard Cordes, Jr.—Son of the militia leader who orchestrated the kidnapping and murder of Samantha's mother.

Marty Flynn—He and Jason served together in the corps. Now they work together in search and rescue.

The mysterious "Buck"—He doesn't care about the ransom money. He just wants Samantha dead.

Prologue

Jason Hunt hung by his fingertips 7,400 feet up in the air. And his phone was ringing.

Another 600 feet and he'd have been out of cell range.

Relying on the strength of his arm, and the sure grip of his hand, he relished the last few milliseconds of silence between each ring. The summer sun was bright overhead, its rays warm on his skin, its heat reflecting off the granite outcropping he'd been scaling for the past hour. Sure, he could have stayed on the marked trail like the tourists, but then he would have missed this view.

Wide-open sky. Miles between this mountain and the next. Snow at the peaks, then silvery-gray granite that gave way to the deep rich greens and browns of the tree line. He even caught a glimpse of Jenny Lake's crystal gray-blue outline from this vantage point. He shifted his grip to swing around the other way, inhaling air that was cooler and cleaner than any part of the world he'd seen. And he'd seen more than he cared to. From here, he could see all the way past the lower peaks into Jackson Hole, the natural valley between the Tetons and Wind River Mountain Range where he'd grown up.

But his phone was ringing.

He eyed the rough granite cliff for the next handhold, doubled his grip of the rock and continued his climb. His next breath wasn't quite as free and calming, but he grounded himself in the unshakable strength of the rock itself and kept moving. These mountains had endured, and he would, too.

He appreciated the quiet of how alone he was between each urgent ring. Save for the wind whistling through the narrow cave a few feet to his left, he'd found the reprieve he needed today. No mortar fire. No grinding of tank and truck gears, no orders to engage or pleas for help shouting in his ear.

Jason found a toehold and pushed himself up another three feet, nearing the top of the rock face. He lived in these mountains. Worked in these mountains. Escaped the memories that time and therapy could never fully erase. He needed the silence. The solitude. The space. No tight quarters here. No small huts or narrow streets filled with fire and booby traps and too many vehicles and people to know his allies from his enemies.

There was no woman dying in his arms up here.

With every ring, Jason's serenity and forgetfulness was shattered. It was a lonely life here in Wyoming. But it was a life.

Until his phone rang.

Mentally bracing himself for the reality of answering that call, he swung himself up over the top ledge.

He shrugged out of the small pack he carried, pulling out both a bottle of water and his cell. The number was no surprise. Neither was the sudden heavy weight of responsibility bearing down on his broad shoulders. With his long legs dangling over the edge into the Teton Mountains' rocky abyss, he swallowed a drink of water and answered his phone. "Yeah?"

"Captain Hunt?"

He pulled off his reflective sunglasses and squirted some of the cooling water on his face before squeegeeing it off his cheeks and beard stubble with the palm of his hand. "We've been stateside for two years, Marty. I told ya you could call me Jase."

"Yes, sir." Marty Flynn was only a few years younger than Jason, and they'd both retired from the Corps once their last stint had ended. But he still spoke to him like the stray puppy he'd first been when he'd been attached to Jason's unit over in the Heat Locker of the Middle East. "Um. Right. Jase."

"What's up, Lieutenant?" Although he already knew. These mountains weren't just his escape now, they were his world.

"Very funny." Yeah. He missed laughter. Not much call to tell jokes when you lived as far off the grid as he did now. "I know it's your day off. Thought you might be locked up in your cabin, shaggin' that pretty girl who was throwin' herself at you at—"

"Talk to me." Like anything resembling a relationship was going to happen after losing Elaine over in Kilkut. Like he'd ever be interested in some brainless twit who couldn't talk about anything but the size of his truck and how hard it was to find sexy clothes at the local boutique. He hadn't wanted to hurt the young woman's feelings when his search and rescue team had stopped at Kitty's Bar in Moose, Wyoming, to toast their commander's pending retirement. She seemed to think getting laid by a veteran Marine was some sort of badge of honor. In his book, it wasn't. He'd left the celebration early. Alone.

"So, you and Lynelle didn't hit it off? You wouldn't mind if I—"

"Marty." Jason exhaled an impatient breath. "*You* called *me*. I assume there's an emergency?"

"Right." Marty might be a natural-born flirt, with more charm than discipline in his repertoire, but he was a damn fine helicopter pilot. He'd saved the lives of Jason and most of his men by flying into an ambush to evac them to the safety of the base. That was the only reason Jason put up with his goofy idol worship—the only reason he'd agreed to take the job with the search and rescue team Marty worked for. He owed him a life. "We've got a missing hiker. Family excursion hiking the String Lake Loop. Little boy wandered off this morning west of Leigh Lake. He's been missing four hours now. Parents searched an hour on their own before calling it in."

Jason climbed to his feet, surveying the mountains in every direction. He assessed the quickest path, the weather, the position of the sun in the sky. "It's already midafternoon."

"And it's summer. Kid doesn't have any bear spray on him. No jacket. Nothing but the clothes on his back. Predators will be out after dark. We need to find him before they do."

Jason tucked the water bottle into his pack and pulled out his vest with a large green search and rescue cross on it. "Or he succumbs to exposure or drowns in the lake."

"You got it. The team's been activated, but we need your expertise in the backcountry. We need you to save the day, big guy."

Right. Because he was so good at that. At least, stateside, nobody had died on his watch.

Jason put on his sunglasses, adjusted the brim of his cap and started moving.

"I'm about fifteen minutes away from the clearing up by Solitude Lake. You can land the chopper there. Come get me. You can drop me at the trailhead, and I'll track the kid from there."

"Will do."

He slipped his search and rescue vest on over his T-shirt and doubled his speed. "Hunt, out."

Chapter One

*Nine months later... The Midas Lodge
outside Jackson, Wyoming*

"Samantha, what are you doing?"

Wishing I was anywhere else.

Hearing her father's tsk-tsking tone above the white noise of conversations, laughter and chamber music drifting in from the reception area of the Midas Lodge's main lobby, Samantha Eddington bit down on the ungrateful thought and stretched up on her toes on the arm of the leather chair she'd pulled from the neighboring window alcove. She closed the back of the mantel clock and screwed the casing shut with her thumbnail before pushing it back into place over the two-story stone fireplace. "Hi, Dad. It stopped at four twenty this afternoon. Fortunately, it was just the batteries." She showed him the oxidized rust stains on the paper napkin wadded up in her hand. "I cleaned them and put them back in, but they won't last for long. We'll need a new set."

Walter Eddington had the build and face of a bulldog, an ironic contrast to the expensive tailored suit and diamond-studded lapel pin he wore. A self-made man who'd served in the Army before Samantha was born, he was as at home in the backcountry with a hunting rifle as he was in the boardroom of the hotel empire he'd purchased on a dare and built into a fortune over the past thirty-five years. Too bad she hadn't inherited either of those skill sets. She didn't share his love for a good party, either, like tonight's shindig that mixed hotel with family business.

But she did love him. Adored him, in fact. After losing her mother when she was seven, they'd become a team—sharing grief and comfort, and helping each other pick up the pieces of their fractured lives. She'd never quite been the tomboy he wanted, nor was she poised enough to serve as the dutiful hostess and helpmate a businessman of his standing needed. And while she understood the numbers and demographics of the lodging and tourism industry, she'd never shared his interest in running a corporation. She loved analyzing the architectural designs and engineering strategies that went into building hotels and resort lodges, but her intellectual acumen and aversion to board meetings, press conferences, and parties like tonight's grand opening celebration with investors and local bigwigs kept her from being the heir he'd hoped for to take over the Midas Group and run the family business one day. Still, Walter Eddington loved her anyway. He was her daddy, the first man she'd loved. And even at twenty-nine, she was his little girl.

"Come down from there." He held out his broad, calloused hand. She took it and smiled as he helped her down from her perch. He dropped a kiss to her cheek, just below the rim of her glasses. "This is supposed to be your party. I realize we're combining business with pleasure by scheduling the grand opening of the new lodge with your engagement announcement to Kyle. But you know how much I want to change the press's perception of you as some kind of eccentric recluse who never recovered from your mother's murder. Hiding out from our guests doesn't help change that image."

"I'm not a recluse. My mind just gets occupied with other things." Too many other things. Like the guilt she felt at putting that worry dimple between his silvering eyebrows.

"I know that," he assured her. "But the last time your picture was on TV and in all the papers, you were only seven. You were so brave. So sad." He captured both hands and backed up to skim his gaze from the loose bun at the nape of her neck to the unpolished wiggle of her bare toes on the woven throw rug in front of the fireplace. He smiled. "You look pretty tonight. All grown up. A woman of the world."

His eyes, the same shade of green as her own, turned wistful. He was losing himself in the past until Samantha squeezed his hands, bringing him back into the present with her. "I miss Mom, too. Tonight of all nights, especially."

Walter nodded, pulling her into his barrel chest and capturing her in one of the bear hugs she'd always loved before he set her back on her feet. He chucked her lightly beneath the chin. "I know you take after my side of the family, but..." He brushed aside a rebellious lock of dark blond hair that had caught in her glasses and tucked it behind her ear. "I see your mother in you tonight. How I wish Michelle could be here to share this with us."

Samantha reached up to straighten the knot of his tie and smooth his lapels, the tender ministrations more of a comfort than a need. "Me, too."

"It's been twenty-two years tonight since that bastard murdered..." Muttering a curse, he blinked away the moisture that glistened in his eyes and pulled something from his pocket. "I want to show you something."

Samantha lit up when she saw the familiar engraved locket on a silver chain that dangled from his fingers. "Mom's necklace. The one you gave her when you got married."

"It'll be yours one day. But tonight, I'm carrying it for luck. That everything goes smoothly, and that Kyle makes you as happy as she and I were. Even if it was for too short a time. I wanted you to know she's with us."

She rubbed her fingertips across the locket's etched surface the way she had as a curious child when it had hung around her mother's neck. Then Walter drew it up to his lips and kissed the heirloom before tucking it back into his pocket. "Don't tell Joyce."

"Don't tell Joyce what?" Samantha's stepmother

appeared behind her father in a swish of pale pink satin. "The party's in the other room, you two." She pointed to the lobby behind them. "Where all the guests are."

With a wink that said he'd cover for Samantha, Walter caught his second wife's hand and kissed her fingers before linking her arm through his. "You'll need to speak to the staging crew, dear. Sammie had to repair this clock. It wasn't working. You know I love the beautiful things you selected to decorate the new lodge. But I expect things to do their job, too."

"Of course I will, dear," Joyce assured him. "I want everything to be perfect tonight."

"I opened it up and cleaned the batteries," Samantha explained.

"Cleaned them with what?" She suspected her stepmother was frowning, although her face revealed little evidence of emotion, one way or another. When Samantha showed her the dirty cocktail napkin, Joyce snatched it from her hand and tossed it into the fireplace.

Unlike Samantha, Joyce knew how to work a room and make a business deal as well as Walter did. His successes were hers and vice versa. Samantha had never quite fit into the family equation the same way after her father had remarried and adopted Joyce's daughter, Taylor. "You are the guest of honor, not maintenance personnel. Are you forgetting that I told the press photographers to be in position at eight? After your father gives his welcoming speech, Kyle will go down on one knee and propose. Just like we rehearsed."

Because nothing says romance like a staged proposal. Samantha scratched at the rash itching beneath the stays of her dress. True, she'd been seeing Kyle Grazer longer than any other man she'd dated—not that there were many names on that list. Being the socially awkward, plain-Jane daughter of a wealthy man like Walter Eddington made it pretty near impossible to trust any man who claimed to be interested in her. But Kyle had persisted. They'd become friends after Joyce had introduced them. Then, her father had offered him a job as an executive in the company, and they'd become something more.

So what if she didn't get the topsy-turvy stomach turbulence she'd expected when she fell in love? Logically, they were good for each other. He helped bring Samantha out of her shell, and she offered him a quiet refuge from the heartache of a girlfriend who'd dumped him and the pain of a father who'd raised him with a harsh, unsympathetic hand. Besides, Kyle was immeasurably patient with her inexperience. He praised her efforts to learn more about kissing and seduction, and promised their lovemaking would improve as she developed more confidence in her relationship skills.

Besides, Grazers came from money. Kyle's father owned a chain of hotels on the East Coast, so she knew he wasn't with her just to get a part of her father's fortune. And her father had assured her more than once that the expected merger of companies that would follow the announcement of their engagement would be negated on the spot if he thought for one moment that Kyle wouldn't take care of her and make her happy. Even if there was something she couldn't quite put her finger on that kept her relationship from being everything she'd hoped for, Samantha *was* happy. Wasn't she?

She rubbed her hand over the hives she'd lived with since her father had asked her to make the engagement a public event and schedule it for tonight—the anniversary of her mother's murder. *"I want to create a positive memory for you,"* he'd said. *"Make this a happy day instead of the anniversary of a nightmare."*

For the company, for her father, for her future—Samantha had every intention of saying yes when Kyle proposed in front of the cameras tonight. This would no longer be the day her mother had been kidnapped and murdered. It would be the day Samantha Eddington got engaged and gave her dad a reason to smile. Now if she could just make the hives go away.

"I didn't forget about the time," Samantha answered, explaining why she'd wandered into the anteroom to fix a broken clock. "Tonight's a big night and I'm understandably nervous. I ran out of small talk after I lost track of Kyle. And the lobby was so crowded, I was getting overheated, so I came out here to check the time, look out the windows and cool off."

"Look out the windows at what? It's pouring down rain out there." Joyce pointed to the bank of floor-to-ceiling windows. "You can't even see the mountains it's so dark."

Samantha crossed to the windows, drawing her finger through the condensation beading there. "You have to admit the rain is cooling things off."

Joyce shook her head, as if the scientific fact made no sense to her. "What do you mean, you lost track of Kyle?" Joyce moved past her husband to straighten the turned-up hem on the embroidered sheer overlay on Samantha's navy blue cocktail dress. "And where are your shoes?" Samantha adjusted her glasses on the bridge of her nose and spied the strappy three-inch heels she'd discarded to climb onto the new resort lodge's furniture. She slipped her feet back into the tan patent leather and fastened the ankle straps, cringing at the sore spots screaming a protest on each of her little toes. "This absentminded professor shtick was cute when you were a teenager, but now it's getting old."

Shtick? Once the wedding was done, Samantha had every intention of becoming a real professor at a reputable university. She'd already earned her PhD. Or, at least she would once she finished her dissertation on the mechanics of waste management design in alpine geographies. If more nights like this one didn't keep her away from her computers and schematic drawings.

"Joyce," Walter chided, joining them. "Ease back on the throttle a bit. This is a big night for Sammie."

"Of course it is. It's a big night for all of us." She batted Samantha's fingers away from her torso when she tried to scratch again. "I've planned everything down to the last minute, from the guest list to the schedule of events to Samantha's dress." A line that could be a dimple or a frown the Botox had missed appeared beside Joyce's mouth. "Why aren't you wearing the red dress Taylor and I picked out for you? She has better fashion sense than both of us put together. It's more photogenic."

For one thing, Taylor was built like a petite fashion model while Samantha was a feminine version of her father's sturdy build. For another, her adopted stepsister's fashion sense reflected the fact that she could wear anything and look like a million bucks, while Samantha was lucky she'd found heels to match her dress. And finally, "Taylor did help me pick this out."

Joyce waved her hand in front of the embroidered flowers covering the A-line dress. "This one is so busy. It's very sweet, but I'm afraid you look more like a girl going to her first communion rather than a woman who's about to get married."

"I like this dress." Couldn't say the same for the three-inch heels of her shoes that chafed her ankles and squeezed all sensation out of her little toes. "Blues and grays are my favorite colors."

"I think she looks lovely," Walter insisted. "Considering she usually wears pants and a lab coat or she's out at a construction site in muddy coveralls, I think she's very dressed up for the occasion."

"You're right, dear. Of course. It is a pretty dress." Joyce's agreeing smile quickly disappeared. "Could you at least put in your contact lenses? Your glasses will reflect the lights when the photographers take pictures." She made a shooing motion with her lacquered fingernails before latching onto Walter's arm again. "Go upstairs and fix yourself. I'll see if I can find Kyle while your father talks to the lieutenant governor." She tilted her face to her father's. "That's why I came looking for you—to tell you she and her husband are arriving."

"Better not keep them waiting." Her father shrugged his big shoulders. Maybe he didn't enjoy these big command performances any more than Samantha did. "I'll see you in the spotlight at eight."

Samantha managed to summon a smile. "I'll be there, Dad."

"Excuse me, sir." A big man with dark hair and a perfectly shaped handlebar mustache walked up behind her father. Dante Pellegrino's muscular bulk was accentuated by the holster and gun he wore underneath his suit jacket. The chief of Midas Group security rarely changed his expression from stoic disinterest, so it was hard to tell when there was an emergency and when he was simply relaying information. "Ma'am. Miss Eddington." He acknowledged Samantha and her stepmother. "Walter? A moment?"

"Is this necessary, Dante?" Joyce asked. "We have a schedule to maintain. Walter is greeting guests until seven forty-five, and then he goes to the podium to make a welcome speech."

"I'm afraid so, ma'am. Something unexpected has come up."

"Very well." Not one wisp of Joyce's silvering blond hair moved as she swung her gaze around, scanning the guests through the open suite of rooms. "I'll stall the lieutenant governor for a few minutes." Even though he was twice her size, she pointed a warning finger at the security chief. "Don't keep him long."

"No, ma'am."

As Joyce bustled away in another swish of stiff satin, Dante whispered in her father's ear. Samantha waited expectantly, wondering if something was happening that would compound her father's worries about this evening's success.

Walter's expression hardened to his time-to-do-business face. "Make sure one of your men stays with Sammie. She's going upstairs for a few minutes."

"Yes, sir."

Samantha tugged on her father's sleeve when he would have pulled away. "Is everything okay?"

"Nothing your old dad can't handle. Don't be late. I want tonight to be all about you." He kissed her forehead and strode away to handle whatever situation Dante had whispered to him.

Either her father didn't think she could understand the problem, or he simply didn't want to worry her. Maybe Dante would be more forthcoming.

She tipped her chin to meet his dark gaze. "What is it?"

He chewed once on the gum that seemed to be perennially in his teeth. Maybe the man had given up smoking, or used the subtle action as a stress-reducing ritual. But since her father had hired his firm a couple of years earlier, she'd never once seen him without the sticky wad in the side of his mouth. "Storm's coming up. There'll be more rain tonight. Snow higher up in the mountains."

She arched a confused brow. "You talked to Dad about the weather?"

"It changes plans."

"What plans?"

"Weather like this brings unexpected guests."

Samantha curved her lips into a wry smile. "We *are* a hotel."

"One that's not open for business yet." Dante gave her a look that lacked any emotion—or any real explanation—as he tapped the radio on his wrist and summoned one of the bodyguards who worked for his security team. "Filly Number One is on the move. Metz? You're up." The bodyguard typically assigned to watch her at public events must have responded in the hearing device wired to the security chief's ear. "Copy that. Pellegrino out."

"Having unexpected guests show up for a party is a security issue?"

"It is tonight." His mustache danced atop his lip as he shifted his gum from one cheek to the other. "It's my job to make sure everything goes as planned. If you're not at that podium at eight o'clock, I'll come get you myself."

Was that a threat? Or just a reminder that she was a commodity in Dante Pellegrino's eyes? Protecting her was no different from guarding the diamond jewelry Joyce and her father were wearing tonight. Grumbling a curse under her breath, Samantha turned and left as quickly as her toe-pinching shoes would let her.

Filly. Although it was a word she was familiar with—she was Number One and Taylor was Number Two when it came to coded security team communications—the nickname only added to her anxiety. She felt like prize livestock tonight, being paraded around for a group of wealthy investors, high-powered executives and gossipy reporters looking for a sensational headline. Joyce was probably hoping that marrying Samantha off would allow her to shift the spotlight over to her own daughter and maybe snag the interest of one of the wealthy guests here tonight to send a son or nephew to come court Taylor. Samantha might have had her fill of socializing, but Taylor would relish all the attention. And she was welcome to it.

Samantha wasn't good enough for her stepmother. She was invisible to the guests. Her father worried too much about her. And she might as well be a horse in the family's stable as far as the security chief was concerned.

"I am so taking a private honeymoon with Kyle," she muttered, hurrying her steps to the trio of elevators. She didn't think her numb toes could handle the staircase up to the mezzanine floor. Even if Kyle wasn't in their room primping for his big moment in front of the cameras, Samantha needed the time away from the people and noise to give herself a

pep talk and get her extrovert on. If she was lucky,
Kyle would be in the room. A few private words and
a kiss would go a long way toward reassuring her
that she was making the right choice in saying yes
to his proposal.

The bodyguard Pellegrino had summoned appeared in the hallway behind her. Brandon Metz
might be the closest thing she had to a friend here
tonight. Even though he was part of the elite security team her father had hired to safeguard the
family and top executives at the company two years
ago, Brandon was usually assigned to her at public
events. Although sworn to be discreet, he knew her
embarrassing idiosyncrasies. He knew she'd rather
be almost anywhere else than dressing up and giving a speech in front of a microphone and flashing
cameras.

Samantha pushed the elevator call button as Brandon's long strides quickly ate up the hallway behind
her. "Samantha?" he called to her as the elevator
dinged and the doors slid open. "What's the hurry?"

If she could get in and close the door before he
caught up to her, he'd be forced to take the stairs up
to the next floor to keep an eye on her. She darted
inside and pushed the button, eagerly anticipating a
whole fifteen seconds or so of peace and quiet.

But Brandon caught the door and stepped into the
elevator with her. "Didn't you hear me?"

She sagged against the back railing. "Sorry. I just
needed a break."

His golden-brown eyes narrowed in a reprimand

that she probably deserved. "I know you're crawling out of your skin dancing through hoops for your family tonight. But it's my job to keep you in my line of sight at all times." Ironically, he turned his back on her, facing the front of the elevator while he spoke into his radio. "Filly One is secure. Heading to mezzanine." He glanced over his shoulder to question her. "The anniversary of your mom's death getting to you?"

"A little," Samantha confessed. Although the grief wasn't as intense as it had been growing up, she still felt the hole in her life that the woman who loved her unconditionally was supposed to fill. But if she started down the trail of all the landmark events in her life her mother had missed, and would miss, then she'd become the weepy little girl pushing her way through a crowd of reporters, asking them where her mother had gone. She was years past allowing herself to be that vulnerable again. A tart tone of sarcasm was one of the defensive tools she'd developed as she'd grown up. "I have to go *fix* myself so I'm up to my stepmother's standards and don't embarrass my father when the paparazzi start flashing pictures."

Brandon chuckled and finished his report as the elevator stopped. "Will keep you posted when she moves again. Yes, I know the timeline," he groused. "Metz out." He held the door and checked the hallway before ushering her out ahead of him and following her to the room she shared with Kyle. "And here I thought you were skipping out on the party to go have a rendezvous with Loverboy."

"I wish." She slipped her hand beneath the hem of her skirt to pull her key card from the leg of her shapewear. "I don't suppose you've seen Kyle the last half hour or so, have you?"

"He's not my assignment."

She slid the card into the lock and opened the door to the faint garble of muffled voices. Maybe Kyle had come up here to catch the market report on the news or listen to one of his motivational podcasts. If he'd abandoned her to watch television or psych himself up for tonight's show, she'd be angry, but at least she'd have an explanation for his disappearance. Samantha nodded to the settee and chairs where the private hallway opened onto a dramatic picture window above the lodge's front entrance. "Relax if you want. I'll only be a few minutes."

He nodded toward the closest chair and side table with its fake potted fern. "I'll give you five minutes. After that, I'll come knockin'." With a lopsided grin, he pulled his cell phone from his suit jacket pocket and retreated into the hallway. She heard him calling someone with another *Filly One* update while she locked the door.

Samantha's deep exhale buzzed her lips as she sagged wearily against the door for a moment. The voices she'd heard had gone silent, so no television. No Kyle, either. She eyed his polished shoes that had been kicked off onto the carpet, and his suit jacket tossed in a lump on the rumpled bedspread beside her purse. Samantha peeked around the corner to knock on the bathroom door. Rumpled was not a typical state for her fiancé. Had he spilled something on him and come up to change? Was he not feeling well? "Kyle? Are you okay?"

The bathroom was empty, and the light was off. The inkling of concern that he might be ill faded. Samantha flipped on the light switch and studied her reflection in the vanity mirror, adjusting her glasses on her pale face before digging through her cosmetics bag to dust on another layer of blush. She was going to have to reach down deep inside her to find the strength and grace to make this evening the success her father wanted it to be.

Once she was sufficiently convinced there was nothing she could do to transform herself into the beauty of the family, Samantha set out her contact lenses and saline solution. But she quickly put her glasses back on when a more proactive way to improve her evening hit her. She returned to the bedroom and sat on the edge of the bed, giving her squished toes a break, and pulled her cell phone from her purse. It would be more efficient to text Kyle and ask his whereabouts than to wander around the ski lodge in hopes of running into him, or trust that he was simply going to show up in the right place at the right time to propose.

After she hit Send, a buzz answered from Kyle's jacket.

Samantha frowned. Even more unusual than Kyle tossing his clothes about was his not having his cell with him. She tugged his jacket into her lap. A black velvet ring box fell from the folds of wool. An unexpected twinge of feminine anticipation made her catch her lip between her teeth as she opened the box. The large marquise diamond surrounded by a double halo of emeralds and tiny seed diamonds was much too gaudy for her tastes. She'd never be able to wear this in the lab or out in the field when she was working. She snapped the box shut, trying not to feel too disappointed by his impractical choice. Why hadn't Kyle bought the simple solitaire she'd shown him?

Since her curiosity had gotten her this far, she didn't hesitate to pull out the folded slip of paper she found in his jacket pocket when she tucked the ring box back inside. This was probably some sappy poem or crib notes he planned to use when he proposed, instead of honest, heartfelt words.

Samantha's jaw dropped open and her breath rushed out as her whole future closed in on her in one humiliating, suffocating moment. She read the names and numbers on the paper. This wasn't even a stupid poem. It was a receipt for the ring. More expensive than she'd imagined. Charged to her stepmother Joyce's account.

"Why would she buy my engagement ring?" If Kyle didn't have the money for that shiny eyesore, then he should have purchased something smaller, more tasteful—a gift from the heart she would have treasured. Had he asked her stepmother to visit the jeweler for him because he'd been away on business so much lately and didn't have time to shop?

She crumpled the receipt in her fist. Maybe this wasn't about the money or time. Were her father and

Joyce that worried about her? She was going through most of this for them. Did they think they were doing all this for *her*? How much of this whole engagement was for the benefit of public relations and the family name? Was any of this marriage bargain real?

Samantha pulled out the velvet box again and squeezed it in her fist. She was sorely tempted to track Kyle down and shove this ring and whatever bargain he thought he'd made with Joyce and her father down his throat.

The whole bed rattled when something thumped against the wall, startling Samantha from her vengeful thoughts. The interruption gave her a moment to temper her emotions, a moment to think more rationally about her discovery. Maybe her own doubts about this engagement were feeding her suspicion of Kyle.

But then she heard the giggle.

Chapter Two

A moment of cold dread was quickly erased by the angry understanding that followed. She should have trusted her instincts. It wasn't the pomp and circumstance of the evening that made her break out in stress hives. It was the idea of marrying Kyle.

When another thump against the wall made her jump, Samantha went to investigate. The door on her side that could be opened to turn the neighboring rooms into one large suite was unlocked and slightly ajar—as was the connecting door into the next room.

She'd like to go back to that whole television- or podcast-watching theory. But Samantha knew better as she pushed the second door open and entered the room that mirrored her own. Though still hushed, she could distinguish the voices and giggles and breathy moans now. She turned past the desk to the closet door, wishing her hearing was as lousy as her myopic vision.

A woman laughed from inside the closet. "Stop shushing me. You said no one could hear us in here."

Oh, how she wished she didn't recognize that voice.

"Just do it, baby. Do it now." Betrayal drove a stake through her heart at Kyle's gasping reply. "Stop talking and…"

Samantha whipped the door open to see Kyle leaning against the closet wall and her stepsister, Taylor, kneeling in front of his unzipped pants.

Oh, hell. Oh, double hell.

Kyle swore.

Samantha watched her stepsister tumble onto her bottom as Kyle pushed off the wall. She backed away, shaking her head.

Taylor's cheeks burned with embarrassment. "Samantha? Oh, my God. I'm so sorry. I never meant to—"

"Screw my boyfriend?" Seriously? Were those tears? "Or just get caught doing it?"

Kyle made a token effort to button his shirt as he stepped out of the closet. "I can explain."

"So can I." Fortunately, he was in a condition that made it difficult for him to hurry after her as Samantha headed to the connecting doors. "Apparently, you lost track of the time. And which sister you're proposing to."

Kyle grabbed her wrist and tugged her around to face him. "Baby, you know I'm committed to you." He captured her by the shoulders, his handsome blue eyes searching hers. Hadn't he just called Taylor *baby*? *Real special endearment, jackass.* "To us. I will see this thing through to the end. I just needed to get this out of my system before we settle down."

"*This?* You mean having sex with my sister?" Samantha twisted in his grasp, and his hold on her tightened painfully.

Taylor scrambled to her feet to follow them, tugging her dress down to her knees. "Out of your system? What does that mean? You said—"

"Shut. Up."

When Kyle turned to dismiss her stepsister, Samantha finally put those three-inch heels to good use and stomped on his stockinged foot, freeing herself. He cursed her and the pain, and stumbled into Taylor. While he teetered off balance, Samantha shoved him back inside the closet, knocking Taylor in with him. The two traitors were falling to the floor, pulling coats and hangers down with them, as she hurled the ring box at them and slammed the door. Tuning out both demands and apologies, she wedged the desk chair beneath the doorknob. Blind with rage and hurt and even a little self-loathing that she hadn't seen this coming, Samantha marched back to her own room and locked the connecting door behind her. She just wanted to escape. If she'd needed a reprieve from the social event downstairs, then dealing with this kind of humiliation demanded nothing less than utter and lengthy solitude.

But she wasn't going to find that here. She spared a moment to pull the luggage rack with her suitcase in front of the door to block the exit, further trapping the two on the other side before grabbing her purse and pulling her checkered trench coat from her own closet.

The argument from the next room continued,

mixed with knocks against the walls and periodic swearing. "You said you were with the wrong sister. That you wanted me. Was that just a line to get me to—?"

"Shut up, Taylor." The doorknob rattled. He pounded on the wall between them. "Samantha, open this door. We need to talk. You're being a child."

And you're being a bastard.

"I love you," he insisted, in the most rote, carefully practiced and insincere tone she could imagine. "I've told you that countless times."

"If only you meant it any one of those times," she muttered before slipping into her black-and-white coat and exiting into the hallway.

She barely noticed Brandon springing to his feet. She hated that her eyes were gritty with tears, hated that she cared enough to hurt like this. But her brain seemed to function, even when her emotions couldn't get their act together. Although Kyle couldn't get to her through the room they'd shared, he'd be able to reach her through Taylor's door. No sense risking that he'd be able to break out of the closet and chase after her. She knocked over the side table, spilling it and the silk fern in front of Taylor's door.

"Um, trouble in Happy Couple Land?" Brandon dodged to one side as she dragged the leather chair in front of the door, building a bigger barricade. "Your mother asked me to remind you—"

"Stepmother, Brandon. Joyce is my stepmother. My real mother died." And apparently, so had any chance at a relationship. After swiping at the tears that clouded her glasses, Samantha booked it down the hallway toward the elevators, leaving the banging and swearing and shouting behind. "Tell Joyce and Dad something came up. I'm leaving."

Brandon stayed right with her. "What did that lowlife do? Is he cheating on you again?"

Samantha stopped in her tracks. "Again? You knew he…? This isn't the first…?" So much for protecting her. She tore her gaze away from the bodyguard's pitying brown eyes and punched the elevator button. *Be angry, not hurt.* "I knew something wasn't right between us. I was trying so hard to make it work. I'm such an idiot."

"Where are you going? I can't let you leave on your own. Especially when you're like this."

"Like what? Awake to reality? Standing up for myself? Saving what little dignity I have left?" The strain of the evening intensified the rash on her torso. Ignoring the habitual urge to scratch, she dug into her purse. "Fine. Then you're coming with me. Here are my keys." She stepped into the elevator, handing them to the confused bodyguard. "Bring my car around back by the kitchen entrance. I'll meet you there. I'm not walking through that lobby and facing all those people again."

"Pellegrino will want to know your destination. He doesn't like changing plans when security is already in place. The rain is pouring—"

"I don't know where I'm going. I don't care if I get wet. I just have to get out of here." She jerked at the crash of splintering wood from down the hallway and punched the first-floor button. "Now."

Brandon grabbed the door to stop the elevator from closing. "What do I tell Pellegrino and your father?"

"Tell them I'm not feeling well. Tell them I'm flying to the moon. I don't care."

"Samantha!" Kyle's shout reached her through the makeshift barriers she'd put up. The closet door was down.

Brandon pulled back his jacket, resting his hand on the gun holstered there. "You want me to stop him?"

At last someone was on her side. But she needed him to do what she needed him to do. "Either get the car right now, or I'm leaving on my own."

He nodded and ran toward the stairs, allowing the doors to close. "I'll meet you under the parking canopy at the kitchen's delivery entrance in back." She could hear him reporting in as the elevator dropped toward the first floor. "This is Metz. Be advised that Filly One is…"

Without even a glance toward the lobby, Samantha hurried toward the kitchen area by one of the lodge's service corridors. With the catering staff out working the party, there was only the chef and her assistant in the kitchen when Samantha pushed her way through the swinging metal door. Ignoring their curious looks and offers to help, she quickened her steps toward the walk-in refrigerator and storage pantry near the back entrance. When the door crashed open behind her and the assistant squeaked in startled surprise, Samantha ran as fast as her aching feet and starched dress allowed.

"Samantha! You have to talk to me."

Kyle hadn't stopped to put on his shoes, and his stockinged feet made no noise as he raced up behind her. She yelped when he grabbed her and spun her around, backing her into a stainless-steel worktable, pinning her there with his hips and hands. His chiseled cheekbones were flushed with exertion, his perfect white teeth clenched as he panted in her face. "I thought you were an adult. Running away is what a child does. You owe it to me to listen."

"I owe *you*?" His fingers clamped down tightly enough to bruise her skin when she shoved at his chest. "Let go of me."

"Clear the room," he ordered the catering staff. When they were too stunned by the argument to budge, he shoved a tray of hors d'oeuvres onto the floor. "Get out!"

Samantha wished she could leave with them as the door swung shut on their backsides. Dishes and pans rattled on the steel table as she squirmed in Kyle's grasp. "You need to let me go."

He released her arms to grab either side of her face, pulling at the pins that held her long hair in place and pinching her scalp, forcing her to look up at him. "You and I are getting married. We have an agreement. Your family likes me."

"Some more than others, apparently."

"Don't get snarky with me. Yes, I screwed up. You have to forgive me."

"Says who?"

"You think there aren't things I would change about you?" he challenged.

How was this her fault? She blinked back the tears that stung her eyes and fought through her emotions to find the words she needed to say. "I'm not the one who's cheating."

"I have a weakness. Okay?"

"No. It's not okay. You didn't even pick out the ring yourself. You couldn't spend that much time on me?"

"I've been busy."

"I can see that."

"With work! I was a little strapped for cash and couldn't afford the ring I wanted to get you, so Joyce helped me out." He was the son of a millionaire and had a good job with the Midas Group. How could he possibly be short of money? Before she could voice the accusation, Kyle touched his sweaty forehead to hers in a supposedly tender gesture, and Samantha wondered how she'd ever found him handsome or charming. "I am committed to us. You know I'm good for you. I help others see beyond the professor and the glasses. We make a good team."

What about needing her? Or wanting her? Or any other stupid compliment that could make her believe he was ever in love with her? The urge to cry disappeared. She let his lips brush against hers, but the moment he thought he was winning her back and his hold on her eased, Samantha twisted from his grasp.

He paused long enough to curse before pursuing her again. "This is a misunderstanding. You need to clue in to how the real world works. I have needs."

She whirled around. "You *need* to keep your pants zipped around other women. If you wanted to get laid, you should have asked me. It's not like I haven't wanted you to…teach me more."

The creep actually smiled. He cupped his fingers against her cheek. "Is that what this is about? Baby, you're too good for a quickie."

She slapped his hand away. "But my sister's not?" She didn't know whether to be flattered or insulted.

"Taylor's young and fun. But she means nothing to me. You mean everything."

"Liar. How many others have there been?"

At least he had the good grace to look guilty. For a split second. Then he was reaching for her again. "Look. Truth. You're learning. Eventually the sex will be great between us, but until you get some confidence—"

She slapped his hand away. "A relationship isn't just about sex. It's about trust and caring and respect. You have no clue—"

When she felt his hand on her arm again, Samantha reached for the first weapon she could find, a heavy skillet resting on the edge of the metal table. She swung around, whacking him in the shoulder. He cursed, grabbing his bruised arm. She knew a moment of guilt, sensing she'd gone too far.

"You are not dumping me." When his eyes narrowed in rage instead of pain, her brain took over.

She had a feeling that escape wasn't just an emotional need at that moment. Shoving the pan into his gut, she forced Kyle back a step. She ordered him to open the refrigerator door. "Get in there. Get in or I swear I'll run straight to my father and tell him you were banging Taylor tonight instead of earning your spot as Midas's newest vice president."

Kyle raised his hands and moved toward her. "You don't want to upset your father tonight…"

"Get in!"

If she'd had any doubts that she was nothing more than a means to an end for Kyle, his willingness to step inside the cooler in exchange for her silence confirmed the truth. As disgusted with herself for being taken in by his promises as she was with the man himself, Samantha closed the refrigerator door and slipped the pin into the lock.

Instead of cursing her or shouting her name, Kyle pulled his cell phone from a pocket and held it up to the window beside his gloating face for her to see.

"How did you…?" Had he broken out through their room? Taken the time to retrieve his phone? Did he have a second cell? Whom was he calling?

Samantha dropped the skillet and opened the back door.

"This is Grazer. I need your help." With the rain beating down on the loading area's metal canopy, she lost the rest of the conversation until he started shouting. "I mean right now! She's taking off. Running out the back door. This *is* plan B!"

Whoever Kyle's ally was, she wasn't waiting for his help to arrive. Slightly breathless with the exertion of fending off Kyle, she scanned the row of employee cars on the other side of the driveway for her silver BMW. The rain fell in sheets on either side of the canopy, blackening the night sky and shrinking her world to the lights beneath the canopy and parked vehicles ahead of her. Her steps stuttered to a halt beside the caterer's van. Where was Brandon? Surely, he'd had time to fetch her car from the lot in front of the lodge to drive back here. "Where are you?"

Although she was out of the elements, the moisture in the air dotted her skin. She shivered with a chill that was part Wyoming springtime and part apprehension. Samantha took out her own phone and pulled up Brandon's number. Should she call him? Give him a few more seconds?

A powerful engine revved nearby. Too big to be her car. Tires screeched against the wet pavement somewhere out in the darkness. Two headlamps came on, their bright lights crystallizing every raindrop, blinding her. Shielding her eyes, Samantha drew back to her side of the driveway so she wouldn't be run over.

Just as she punched in her bodyguard's number to get her out of this madhouse, a black van erupted from the wall of rain and skidded to a stop only feet away, sending a wave of dirty water splashing over her feet. "Hey!"

The side door opened and two men in dark camouflage gear and ski masks jumped out. One was carrying what looked like a machine gun.

Samantha screamed.

"Shut her up!" a growly voice ordered.

She spun around and slammed into a third man. Where had he come from? Strong arms snugged around her like a vise, knocking the phone from her hand. "Let go of me!"

"Get that phone!" someone shouted.

Someone tore her purse off her shoulder. She kicked. Clawed. Twisted. "Brandon! Help! Help me! Ky—!"

A gloved hand slapped an oily cloth over her mouth and nose, forcing her to breathe in some nasty fumes, making her dizzy. Rough hands lifted her off her feet. Her knee cracked against the running board of the van before she was shoved inside. "Help me," she wheezed. The hands let go and she rolled across the floor of the van, slamming into the opposite side. "What's happening? Who are you?"

"Samantha!" Help. Brandon was coming for her. She heard two sharp pops, and jumped inside her skin at the metallic clank of two bullets striking the back of the van.

A man in the front seat thrust his hand out the window and fired a gun that made a whup, whup sound. A silencer. Her would-be rescuer wouldn't hear the man returning fire.

She pushed herself up, tried to warn him. "Brandon!"

The side door slammed shut. The van lurched forward and she fell.

"Glasses."

Cruel hands pulled them off her face, blurring the world around her. "Please... I can't see—"

"I said shut her up." She felt the prick of a needle in the side of her neck. "Get the tracking device." The man giving orders cursed. "Drive!"

Those same cruel hands tugged at her coat. A sharp blade pierced the back of her shoulder. Her world blurred into a woozy haze of faceless men and squealing tires.

Kidnapped. Just like her mother. Michelle Eddington had been taken on a raw night just like this one.

Samantha's brain went dark on one final thought.

Kyle's betrayal, seeing his daughter used and being played for a fool himself, might anger her father.

But this would break him.

Chapter Three

A beer bottle sailed through the air. Jason dodged the flying projectile and watched it shatter against the wood door frame behind him at Kitty's Bar.

He halted a moment to brush off some of the beer that had sprayed his jacket and quickly assessed the combatants of the fight he'd just walked in on. Looked like locals versus outsiders. Located on the outskirts of Moose, Wyoming, Kitty's was usually a quiet hole-in-the-wall where a man could get a drink and meet a friend without running into too many people. But at o-dark-thirty on a Friday night, this place had more people in it than he'd ever seen—and half of them were throwing punches.

"Stop it!" Kitty Flynn yelled from behind the bar as a table tipped over, spilling playing cards and poker chips over the warped floorboards.

He spotted a familiar search and rescue ball cap sliding across the floor before zeroing in on a head of curly red hair. Sure enough, Marty Flynn, Kitty's nephew and Jason's coworker, was right in the middle of it, landing a punch on a blond guy in a three-piece suit before pulling a dark-haired waitress out of Blondie's arms and pushing her toward the bar and his aunt. "You get out of there, Cathy, before you get hurt."

Marty shoved at a dark-haired twenty-something wearing jeans and a flannel shirt. That was one of the Murphy boys, twins who ran a gun shop with their dad. He never could tell Cy and Orin apart. The kid shoved right back, trying to get at a tall, lanky man who already sported a black eye. Jason pulled off his knit cap and shook the rain from the dark hair that dripped onto his collar. He never should have answered his phone.

"Hey, Captain. I've got a woman we need to track down in the Tetons."

"Missing hiker?" Jason had asked, thinking the woman was a fool to risk going up into the high country in the spring before the upper elevations had thawed. But he was already grabbing his go bag to load into his four-wheel-drive truck. Night was the worst time to be lost in the mountains. And all this rain and snow, depending on where she was on the mountain, made this a particularly miserable night.

"Not exactly." Either the woman needed their help, or she didn't. Jason waited for the younger man to explain. "Meet me at Aunt Kitty's place. I'm not calling in anybody else on the S&R team because the guy who wants to hire us says this rescue needs to stay off the books. Hell, I'm not even filing a report with the boss, just getting clearance for a flight plan

from the airport. I don't think we need anybody else. And we could make some good money. A lot of it."

Jason didn't care about the money. What he cared about was living with his conscience. Letting another woman die when he could do something to help was his Achilles' heel. Letting anyone die in those mountains when he knew them better than just about anybody in a hundred-mile radius wasn't something he could hide away from, although he tried damn hard to hide from the world as much as it would let him. He'd found that five-year-old kid who'd wandered off from his parents last summer. He'd tracked down a mountain biker who'd had a run-in with a cougar, carried the guy on his back to clear ground so he could be life-flighted to the hospital. There'd been skiers and snowboarders who'd needed his help, and he'd been there, too, for them.

But it was never enough. The debt was still there. He'd lost too many lives over in Kilkut. No matter how far off the grid he got, that need to balance the scales—a life for a life—demanded that he answer Marty Flynn's call. Maybe one day the score would be even, and the losses he'd suffered in the Corps, the anger and the guilt, wouldn't be able to find him anymore.

And so, he was here. At Kitty's Bar on the outskirts of Moose after midnight, walking into the middle of a bar fight.

Looked like Marty was actually trying to stop the fight, and was getting cursed and dinged up for his trouble. Four more locals, judging by their boots and jeans like Jason wore, were going after four guys in suits who seemed to be toying with them. One of the suits, an older man with a square face and silvering hair, hung back behind the tall guy and a bruiser with a handlebar mustache. Although he seemed mature enough to avoid duking it out with men half his age, he wasn't above shouting orders, or answering taunts about getting the hell out of where he didn't belong. Mustache Man had training. He blocked every punch, braced his feet when another drunk local charged him and used his attacker's momentum to shove him off to the side.

Blondie wiped a trickle of blood from his mouth and grabbed the older man's arm, pulling him away from two men who knocked over a bar stool and toppled to the floor. "Stay out of it, Walter. Let the professionals handle these yokels. That's what you pay them for."

"I'm not afraid of a fight." While the older man didn't dive into the thick of swinging arms and wrestling men, he did shrug off the young man's grip, stepping forward while Blondie waved him off with a dismissive curse and pulled out his cell phone.

Marty looked a little outnumbered, since neither side seemed interested in backing down. But Jason's priority was the missing hiker, not bailing Marty out of a tough situation because someone had made a joke with the wrong person, or the city dude had made a move on one of the small-town country girls.

Sure, Jason could handle himself in a fight. The Marines had trained him to do that better than most.

And the fact that he was built like a tank and stood almost a head taller than anyone else in the room generally dissuaded all but the drunkest or most stupid from picking a fight with him in the first place.

But he didn't wage war anymore. Only the one inside his head. Not even for a friend from the Corps. Jason backed toward the broken bottle and swinging door. Marty could call in a different favor on another day.

Jason was big, but he wasn't fast. Not fast enough to make his escape, at any rate.

"Captain! Jason. Thank God. This is the—" Another local boy with a dark crew cut and tats lunged past Marty, trying to get at the old man. He recognized Richard Cordes Jr., the son of a militia leader who'd led a remote compound in the area back when Jason had been a boy. "Damn it, Junior, I said back off!"

"Mind your own business, Marty." More glass smashed. "Eddington!"

"Jase!"

Putting every emotional survival instinct on hold, Jason squeezed his eyes shut, inhaled a deep breath and answered Marty's plea for help.

He grabbed the young man who was picking himself up off the floor and shoved him down in a chair with a warning to stay put. Kane Windisch—he was Junior Cordes's cousin. Jason captured the next punk in a neck hold and twisted him out of his path to reach Marty and Junior, who was wielding a broken bottle, ready to cut anyone who got too close.

And that's when he saw the guns. The bulges inside their suit jackets indicated Mustache Man and the lanky suit guy already sporting a black eye were both carrying.

"You shouldn't have come here at all, old man," Junior whined. The young hotshot poked the jagged edge of the bottle at the old man who must be Eddington. Mustache Man pulled back his jacket and reached for his gun. "Accusing me of stuff you know nothin' about."

As Junior lunged forward, Jason grabbed him from behind, lifting him off his feet and trapping his arms at his side, shaking him until his grip popped open and he dropped the bottle. Jason kicked it aside and set Junior down. The kid reeked of beer and smoke, like he'd just come in from camping. Jason shoved him back and pointed a warning finger at him. "You need to sober up and calm down."

Junior smacked his hand away. "Get out of my face, Jase."

"Who are you supposed to be?" Mustache Man sneered from behind him. "The cavalry? We got this covered."

Jason turned on him next, unused to looking men straight in the eye, but not fazed by the man's size, either. He nodded to the gun in his hand. "You need to put that away."

"And he needs to back off," Mustache Man warned.

"These boys aren't armed." No telling how many rifles and shotguns Junior and his buddies had stowed in their trucks outside. But Jason figured

Mustache Man already knew that. This guy was a pro, former military if not a trained bodyguard for the old man and Blondie. Like Jason, he probably even knew about the revolver Kitty kept behind the bar for protection and to break up fights like this melee. But that didn't mean Jason would allow him an unfair advantage over a group of young men who were too plastered to think straight. "I said put it away."

"You ain't fightin' any fights for me, Jase." Jason heard Junior squirming against the restraining grip Marty and one of the twins had on him. "I ain't afraid of you, Eddington, or your peacekeepers you brought with ya."

"Dante." The silver-haired man in the pricey suit put a hand on Mustache Man's shoulder. "Put the gun away." But his eyes were fixed at a point beyond Jason's shoulder. "I've been watching you for two years now, Mr. Cordes, and I've been content to keep my distance. As far as I'm concerned, justice was served the day of your father's execution. But if you've done anything to my daughter, I will make it my business."

Junior's lips buzzed with a beer-fueled curse. "Justice, my ass." He elbowed Marty in the gut, freeing himself. "You here to take my land, too? The way you took my daddy's?" He charged the older man. "You'll see how we do justice around these parts."

Dante was definitely Eddington's protector. The big man moved forward to block Junior. With barely a twitch of his mustache, he twisted Junior's arm behind his back, pushing him into the dark-stained pinewood bar and smashing his face down onto the polished bar top.

One of the twins lunged forward to help his buddy. But he pulled up short, raising his hands in surrender as Mustache Man pulled his gun and aimed it squarely at the young man's face.

"Back off," Mustache Man warned.

Enough. Jason pulled the young man out of harm's reach and stepped forward to take his place. The gun was now pointed at his chest, but it didn't waver as Mustache Man's dark eyes narrowed.

"Take a deep breath, mister," Jason stated in a calm voice. The other suit had pulled his gun, too. An MK-23. He hadn't seen a laser-sighted pistol since his last deployment. Didn't know why any man would need hardware like that stateside. These two meant business.

Mustache Man pushed a little harder on Junior's skull to keep him pinned to the bar. The damn gun didn't move. "You are outmatched, my friend. There are two of us, and you're not armed. I am Dante Pellegrino, owner of Pellegrino Security."

"Good for you." Jason wasn't impressed by the posturing.

"Yo, Jase." Marty Flynn materialized at Jason's side, dusting off his cap and plunking it backward on his head. "This is Jason Hunt, Mr. Eddington. The guy I told you about. Served with him in the Corps."

"Dante." Like a superior officer, the bulldog who answered to *Mr. Eddington* spoke to his man in a tone that said he expected him to listen. "Let Cordes go. I need to talk to this man. Put your gun away. Brandon, you, too."

With a deliberate chomp on the gum or chew he held in his cheek, Pellegrino released Junior and holstered his weapon. His sidekick did the same. When Junior sprang toward Pellegrino, Jason tripped him and shoved him out of harm's way, warning him to walk away from the fight before Jason chose a different side.

"You, too, Kitty." Jason's tone was a little more indulgent with the barkeep, since she reminded him of the mother he hadn't spoken to in two years.

"Jason Hunt, if you didn't look so much like your daddy…" With some noisy grousing about people telling her what to do in her own place, she circled back behind the bar and put the revolver away in its drawer. "Cathy, get the broom and dustpan out of the back room." The young waitress eagerly hurried off to do her boss's bidding. "Wash your face while you're back there, too."

"Yes, ma'am."

Only after the weapons were all accounted for did Jason take his eyes off Pellegrino. He glanced over to where Junior was downing a surviving shot of some dark liquor and grinning like an idiot. "Go on home." He nodded to his cohorts who were already gathering their jackets and hats. "One of you sober enough to drive?"

One of the twins—Orin, he thought—nodded.

He'd been the one with the gun shoved in his face. He shrugged into a lined denim jacket. "Yes, sir."

But Junior had been the son of a fiercely independent militia leader. In addition to inheriting his father's rebellious attitude toward all things authoritarian, he was a little too drunk to choose keeping his mouth shut and leaving as the wiser course of action. He adjusted his stained and twisted cowboy hat over the crown of his head. "You owe me, Eddington. You owe my family. You don't know who you're messin' with."

Kitty circled around the bar with a tray and wet rag to clean the messy table. "Please, Junior, just go. Drinks are on the house. Whatever beef you've got with these people—"

"You don't need to do me any favors. I ain't so broke that I can't pay my debts." He tossed a couple of bills onto the table before turning to volley one last shot. "You took my daddy from me, Eddington. You watch out or I'll take something from you."

"Damn you, Cordes." The older man surged forward. "If you've harmed my daughter in any way… I'll give you the money right now if it means getting her—"

"You can't give him the cash." Pellegrino moved to intercede, but Jason hooked his arm around Pellegrino's shoulder to stop him from turning this argument into another fight, especially when Kitty would be caught in the middle of it. Pellegrino sloughed off Jason's hold and bounced a warning glare from his dark eyes.

Kitty stepped in front of the older man. "I told you, Junior has been here all night, playing cards. He couldn't have taken your daughter."

Taken? That word left a very bad taste in Jason's mouth. What had Marty gotten him into?

"I'm goin', Kitty. I'm goin'." With his posse urging him toward the door, Junior put on his jacket. He paused when he brushed past Jason's shoulder, looking up as though seeing him for the first time. "I could have taken him, you know." No, he couldn't. Not with the buzz on that clouded his judgment and coordination. Not against firepower like Pellegrino and his man were carrying. "You talk to your daddy recently? You're lucky you still can. I heard Nolan's been to see the doctor a couple of times this last month. You ought to call home sometime, instead of spending all your days building that cabin up in the woods. Or interferin' with my business."

A flash of concern that Jason's father, Nolan Hunt, was facing some kind of health scare he didn't know about blindsided Jason for a split second. He was equally steamed that Junior had chosen to make his screwed-up life *his* business, just because his pride was wounded. But Jason quickly shoved both emotions back where they belonged, relaxing the fist at his side. There was a reason Jason was out of the loop on family matters, a reason why he chose the wide-open space of the mountains over life in Jackson, Wyoming, where his parents lived. And no taunt from a drunken kid was going to make him forget that reason.

"Good night, Junior. Stay out of trouble."

After the door swung shut on Junior and Orin, the older gentleman in the three-piece suit stepped up to shake his hand. "Mr. Hunt. I'm Walter Eddington. Thank you for coming on such short notice. What'll you drink?"

Kitty scooped up her tray and headed back to the bar. "I'll get a fresh pot of coffee brewed for you, Jase, and bring you a cup."

He nodded his thanks and followed Marty and Eddington to join the blond man who'd left the fight to make a call at a large, stained table at the far side of the bar. He hung back when Dante Pellegrino and his sidekick flanked him, refusing to come any closer until they gave him the space he needed. Pellegrino smoothed his thumb and forefinger over the curves of his mustache, sending Jason a very clear message that he was used to calling the shots around his employer. But with Jason not budging, Walter Eddington muttered a choice word and ordered Pellegrino to take a seat. Before obliging his employer, he shifted his gaze to his hireling and nodded toward the bar's front door. "Metz. Check outside to make sure Cordes and his boys drive away and don't come back. I don't want any surprises."

"Yes, sir." As the younger man buttoned his suit jacket and jogged toward the door, the ladies' room door opened in the back and the drama of the evening took a turn into Circus Land.

Two women who looked as out of place in this beer-scented joint as daisies in a patch of weeds came out of the ladies' room. A twenty-something blonde in a shiny silver dress wheeled out a duffel-shaped overnight bag, while an older, equally dolled-up version of sophisticated beauty murmured something dismissive into the cell phone at her ear. The older woman met Jason's assessing gaze before ending her call. While Marty pulled out a chair for the young woman, the mature blonde sat next to Eddington at the head of the table. "I'm assuming it's safe to bring the money back out now that Mr. Cordes and his unpleasant friends are gone?" She squeezed his hand. The proprietary gesture and white gold band of diamonds on her hand told Jason they were husband and wife. "Are you certain they have nothing to do with Samantha?"

"I'm not certain of anything anymore." Eddington pulled her hand to his lips to kiss it. She reached over to brush a strand of silver hair off his forehead with a lacquered fingernail. The tender gesture drew attention to the older man's weary expression. His skin had been ruddy with emotion during that stand-off with Cordes, but now his face had a gray quality to it, as if the toughness he'd summoned for that confrontation at the bar had faded away. "Mr. Hunt, this is my wife, Joyce. My younger daughter, Taylor. And I don't believe you met Kyle Grazer. He works for me at the Midas Hotel Group. He was supposed to become my future son-in-law tonight."

"Supposed to?" Grazer paused in the middle of pulling out a chair beside the younger woman. "Nothing has changed in my plans for Samantha.

They've only been delayed." He picked up the heavily packed duffel bag and dropped it into the middle of the table, rattling every glass and earning a glare from the older man. "This isn't even what they asked for. Screw your principles. If we do what they tell you, we'll get her back. Otherwise——"

"Kyle." Joyce Eddington shot him a look that forced the young man into his seat. Clearly, the woman was very protective of her husband. But the outburst triggered a gasp and a sniffle from the young woman. Joyce tutted a reprimand behind her teeth, but put an arm around her daughter's shoulders. Jason suspected that one reason for the trip to the bathroom had been for Taylor Eddington to apply a fresh coat of makeup to mask the puffiness around her red-rimmed eyes. "Taylor, dear, I need you to be stronger than this. Kyle, we need your handkerchief."

When he hesitated, Marty pulled a blue bandanna from the pocket of his jeans and held it out to the petite blonde, sliding into the empty chair across from her. The young woman slid a quick glance up to Grazer's glaring expression before softly thanking Marty and dabbing at the moisture on her face. "I'm all right, Mother. I'm just worried about how Samantha is doing. She must be so frightened. And we're still sitting here, talking about what we should do when she might already be——"

Joyce squeezed her hand, shaking her head to keep her daughter from finishing that sentence.

Before anyone else snapped or glared or cried, Jason reached over the table to unzip the bag. He didn't have to open it very far to see the bundles of cash packed inside. Ransom. A far cry from a cache of high-tech weaponry and intelligence info, but the bargaining chip was the same—a woman's life.

His blood scalded like acid in his veins at the vivid memories he couldn't escape. He wasn't sure he could do this again. Marty thought they were going to make some easy money. He had no idea what he'd signed them up for. How much it could cost them if they failed.

But once a Marine, always a Marine. Jason was hardwired to be mission-oriented, and a shot at redemption was as tempting as it was unsettling. He closed the bag and pulled out a chair, swinging it around to straddle it beside Walter Eddington. "Who's been taken?"

"Straight to the point. I like that. I'm a military man myself. Served a stint in the Army back in Vietnam." For a brief moment, Walter Eddington looked truly old. But with a deep breath that expanded his barrel chest, he pulled out his phone and slid it across the table in front of Jason. "This was texted to me at midnight. My older daughter, Samantha."

Eddington turned away, unable to watch the screen. He pulled a silver chain from his jacket pocket, running his thumb over every link as if he was counting rosary beads. That wasn't a good sign. Jason's jaw tightened as he took the phone and played the video message.

Hands that belonged to unseen men plucked a black hood off a woman's head. She put her bound wrists up to her face and squinted against the sudden brightness of the lights shining on her, lights that also obscured her captors and their surroundings. Long ash-blond waves tumbled down one side of her neck while straighter strands still caught beneath hairpins floated upward with static electricity. When the gloved hands pulled her arms away from her face, she winced, but didn't cry out.

An off-camera voice muttered something unintelligible and she blinked open big green eyes. She ran her tongue across her full bottom lip and cleared her throat, as if she was thirsty and struggling to speak. "I can't even see the camera without my glasses, much less read that scrawl of yours."

"Give 'em to her," the muffled voice ordered.

She glanced blindly about until the gloved hands reappeared and thrust a pair of tortoiseshell-framed glasses onto her face. As Samantha Eddington blinked the world into focus, she whispered a soft "Thank you."

Jason fought the urge to bolt. This was Kilkut all over again. The hair and eye color might be different, but with those glasses, she looked too much like… The memory of a bullet hole through the shattered lens of a woman's glasses superimposed itself over Samantha Eddington's face. He curled his fingers into a fist, fighting off the past and focusing squarely on the present reality of those big green eyes.

"Say it." The harsh voice wasn't muffled now.

Samantha nudged her glasses into place and looked into the camera. "Dad? Um, I got myself into some trouble here. Never should have left that stupid party. I'm so sorry. Is Brandon okay? He tried to help. I know you're thinking about Mom right now. I felt like I needed to get away before I exploded, but I never thought any of this—"

"Cut the sentimental crap and read it."

"Will you take me to use the outhouse if I do? My bladder's about to bust."

Her answer was the distinctive sound of a bullet sliding into the firing chamber of an automatic handgun. "Read it."

Her green eyes widened and locked on to someone off camera beside her, no doubt holding a gun on her. Samantha Eddington was pale, scared, dressed in some nonsense fancy dress that curved over her generous breasts and left her visibly shivering. Or maybe that was fear. But other than the edge of a bandage peeking out beneath the flowery strap over her left shoulder, at least she didn't appear to be injured.

She turned her focus to something at the right of the camera and started reading. "We—these men, of course, not me—want five million dollars. Wow. That's a million dollars apiece. You must think—"

"Stop ad-libbing." The barrel of the Sig Sauer pointed at Samantha entered the camera shot, inching closer to her caramel-blond hair. "Word for word."

Although this was hard to watch, Jason was learning more about the situation in the few seconds he watched the nearsighted socialite on camera than he'd learned in the previous few minutes with the rest of her family and employees. At least five men,

armed with pricey hardware, were holding her someplace that had an outhouse. So not in town, and not
anyplace where a military-grade weapon like that
would be noticed. There were snowflakes dotting
the black camouflage material on the arm holding
that weapon. Snow meant they were at a higher el-
evation. Samantha Eddington was smart—maybe a
little too clever for her own good if her kidnappers
caught on to all the clues she was dropping and pun-
ished her for it.

With a jerky nod, she lowered her gaze to the
script. "If you don't pay us the money, you'll lose
your daughter…" She hesitated, twisting her lips into
a frown, blinking back tears before reading on. "…
just like you lost your wife. I'm sorry, Dad. I know
how hard this is for you. If anything happens to me,
promise me you won't blame—"

"Read it!" The gun ground against her temple
and she froze.

Tilting her head away from the gun, she continued. "We'll call tomorrow morning at eight with an
account number where you will deposit the money.
Once the deposit has cleared and we're out of the
country, we'll call again and give you Samantha's location. If the money isn't there by noon, all you will
find is her body." A delicate muscle rippled down her
throat as she swallowed again. "Unless…the scav-
engers find her first." She shook off the terror that
threat must engender and read on. "No cops. No
FBI. Don't send your fancy security force after us.
It's time to pay up. Five million for your daughter's

life." Her green eyes darted toward the camera. "I tried to fight them, Dad. But my toes are freezing up here. Remember when you tried to teach me how to hunt? I wish I had that gun now—"

"Shut her up."

The gloved hands whisked the glasses off her face. "Please, don't. I read what you wrote. You don't understand what my father's been through. He won't pay—"

"He damn well better."

She was struggling with her captors now. And losing. The men pushed her down to the floor and the camera followed.

"Stop! Please… No!"

"We'll kill her if you don't cooperate, Eddington," an off-screen voice promised.

Another pair of hands pushed her loose hair off her face, exposing her long, creamy neck to the syringe they held. She grimaced when the needle pricked her skin. Her words were already slurring as she looked toward the camera. "I love you, Dad."

The screen went black before a cue icon beckoned Jason to replay the disturbing images. But he'd already memorized any useful intel he could get off the video. His blood simmered as experiences from the past were already painting a dark outcome for Samantha Eddington's future. He'd put his fist through the table if he watched it again. If he couldn't block these emotions, he'd be no use to anybody. And clearly, Samantha desperately needed somebody's help. His kind of help.

But Jason wasn't sure he was mentally fit to handle this kind of dark ops rescue mission anymore. He handed the phone back to Samantha's father. "You got five million dollars?"

"I do."

"Pay the ransom." He rose from his chair, giving the best advice he could, even as he tried to save his sanity and make an exit.

"I won't give in to their threats." Eddington was sentencing his daughter to death on some kind of principle? The older man stood to block Jason's path to the door. "You may not know who I am, Captain Hunt, but this isn't the first time I've gone through this. I paid a million dollars to Richard Cordes and his militia for my wife Michelle twenty-two years ago. The kidnappers killed her, anyway."

Twenty-two years ago, Jason had been a middle-schooler, discovering girls weren't icky, counting the days until his father returned from his latest deployment and not paying attention to the news. But even now, he had a glimmer of a memory about the dead woman who'd been found in a gully outside Cordes's militia compound. He glanced over to the table where Richard Jr. had been playing cards. "You came here to accuse Junior of taking your daughter?"

"Yes. He and I were both there the day his father was executed for Michelle's murder. He said things… I know he blames me for his father's death. He thinks I cheated his family when I bought the militia's land to build a ski resort. Of course, they didn't own it. They were squatters who'd taken over government land. I had a legal deed and I paid a fair price for every acre. But I'm sure that's what his father preached to him his entire life. I didn't want to argue with him. I just wanted—"

"Samantha back." Joyce rose beside her husband as his shoulders sagged. She took over the conversation when Walter couldn't immediately continue. She dragged the duffel bag across the table. "I told Walter we should come prepared to make a deal. He scraped together over a hundred grand in cash. But Mr. Cordes was insulted by the offer. Of course, he was also drunk and hitting on my daughter."

"Mother." Taylor Eddington seemed embarrassed to be any part of this conversation.

Kyle Grazer, however, didn't seem to have any problem making himself heard. He pounded the table with his fist. "Pay the damn ransom, Walter! All of it. Your stubbornness is going to get her killed."

The accusation galvanized the older man. His cheeks flushed with anger as he pushed his wife aside and met the younger man nose to nose. "You have no say in this. If you had stayed by Samantha's side tonight—"

"I'm the one who tried to stop her from leaving."

Taylor burst into tears and dashed off to the bathroom while Joyce Eddington urged the two men to behave like gentlemen and Pellegrino inserted his shoulder between them and forced Grazer back a step. The younger man tipped his chin up to the mustachioed bodyguard and swore. But, as Jason suspected he would, Grazer backed off.

Pellegrino's dark eyes never left Grazer's as he put the microphone on his wrist up to his lips and called his man back inside. "Metz? If the coast is clear, I need you in here to walk Mr. Grazer out to the limo."

"Save your damn escort," Grazer whined. "You can afford to lose five million, Walter. Can you afford to lose anyone else you love? If anything happens to Samantha, it's on your head." He pulled out his cell phone and stalked toward the bar's swinging door, exchanging a sour glance with Brandon Metz on the way out as the younger bodyguard came in.

Metz shrugged in confusion, but joined them at the table when Pellegrino waved him over. "Grazer can walk it off." He reached for the duffel bag of cash. "I need you to secure this."

"Yes, sir."

But Eddington was taking charge again. He pulled the duffel bag from Pellegrino's hands and shoved it into Jason's chest. "Mr. Flynn says you're the best. Consider this a down payment. I'll give *you* the five million if you bring Samantha home alive."

Pellegrino immediately intervened, taking the bag back into his custody. "Whoa, Walter. I said my men and I would go after Samantha. This guy will be our guide. You can't pay some stranger to rescue her."

"The message said specifically not to send you. No cops, no FBI."

Mrs. Eddington wasn't about to be left out of the argument. "I think Kyle is right. We should pay the ransom. Make sure Samantha is safe. Then worry about bringing these men to justice."

Walter raised his voice. "I want her home before the next phone call. Before it's too late."

Jason shot a look across the table, catching the wry apology on Marty Flynn's face. Damn Marty for getting him involved with this. But he couldn't walk away. He couldn't live with another Elaine Burkhart on his conscience.

"I'll do it."

His nostrils flared with a deep breath as he summoned the years of training in both the military and search and rescue that lived inside him. Those skills triggered the muscle memory and do-or-die mindset that turned him into a man he didn't want to be anymore. But he had to become that man to do this job, to salvage his conscience, to save an heiress with pretty green eyes so he'd be able to sleep at night. "I need to know everything about your daughter's abduction, and an explanation for those clues she was feeding us on that video." Jason felt a clock ticking now. Whatever needed to be done would have to happen within the next few hours, before the 8:00 a.m. deadline. "Did you take Samantha hunting? Stay at a cabin with an outhouse?"

"She didn't have the right shoes on that trip." With Jason's urging, Eddington processed the information from the video. "When she was twelve, I took her up past Marion Lake and showed her how to use a gun. She didn't want to aim at any of the birds we were after, but she'd shoot at a paper target. She liked the mechanics of the weapon. My girl always did like to tinker with gadgets and fix things. Sammie spent more time taking her rifle apart and cleaning it than she did with any actual hunting. I'd rented a cabin for the weekend. She was tucked in and asleep by the fire before I realized she'd worn her tennis shoes instead of the boots I'd got her. Her feet were soaked and her toes like ice before I got her warmed up."

"Where was that cabin?"

"On the trail going up to Teton Canyon." Walter shook his head. "That place was torn down six years ago. They can't be holding her there."

"But if she's familiar with that area, that could be the connection she was making." The national park alone covered 485 square miles. It was imperative that they narrow down the search area if there was any chance of rescuing Samantha before the kidnappers called again. "There are supply cabins and a handful of rental properties all along that trail. The kidnappers could be holed up in any one of those."

"At the time that video was made," Pellegrino pointed out. "They could have moved on."

And she could already be dead. A plan was forming in his head, but Jason needed to get up to speed as quickly as possible. He wasn't going to wait until it was too late to go after Samantha Eddington. Even if this mission had been forced upon him, he wasn't going to have another hostage rescue gone to hell because somebody else kept him from doing his job. "How did they get their hands on her?"

"That's on me." Brandon Metz glanced at the door before answering. "I was waiting for Grazer to come clean. But since he weaseled out… The two of them had a blowup, and she decided to leave instead of going back to the party." He exhaled a rueful sigh. "I'm pretty sure there's not going to be an engagement."

"That son of a bitch had the nerve to sit here at this table—"

"Walter." Joyce Eddington interrupted her husband before he sprang from his chair. "We don't know what happened yet. We'll straighten things out with Kyle. We might need his help with Samantha."

The long-limbed bodyguard gave a reluctant nod. "Grazer was the last person to see her. He said she lost her temper, was behaving irrationally. He called the security team for help."

Pellegrino confirmed as much. "I'm the one who let him out of the walk-in freezer where she'd locked him up."

The woman had fire. She'd have to in order to survive this bunch. She was resourceful, too, if she could end an argument with the other guy locked up. And even with a gun to her head, there'd been nothing random about the intel she'd fed them on that video.

But any awareness of those haunting eyes or admiration for his target's intelligence would be distractions that could derail this mission. "Get back to the abduction."

Metz continued. "Men were waiting for us in the parking lot."

"They ambushed you?" With something as spontaneous as an argument to drive her out of the lodge, away from witnesses, the abduction indicated inside knowledge of Samantha and the people around her, or someone monitoring her movements. Like a fiancé. Or a family member. Or a bodyguard.

"The rain masked their approach. Two men pulled me out of the car. I put up a fight, but they knocked me out, removed my weapon. I grabbed my spare sidearm out of the glove compartment as soon as I could get to my feet, but they fired on me. The shots came from a black van. I managed to get off a couple of shots before they turned west onto Highway 22. I called it in to Pellegrino and went after them."

"Heading into the Bridger-Teton National Forest." Jason knew the area well. But that was still a lot of miles to cover in a search for the missing woman. "You get a plate number?"

"A partial." Metz gingerly tapped the swelling at his temple. "My vision was a little out of focus."

Pellegrino dismissed his employee. "Go outside and keep an eye on Grazer. He's a loose cannon. I don't trust the guy."

"Sir, I want to be part of the team that goes after her," Metz argued. "She was taken on my watch."

"Outside. Now."

Metz's mouth opened as if he wanted to respond to that directive. But he wisely snapped it shut and headed for the exit. "Yes, sir."

Pellegrino watched his man leave before taking over the briefing. "You can't blame him. These guys are pros. Samantha's cell signal went dead around the time she was taken. The kidnappers used a burner phone we can't trace."

"You thinking of hiking up to the high country tonight, Jase?" Marty finally added his voice to the conversation. "I can't fly the chopper and do a visual search until sunrise. That's still a lot of ground to cover before that eight o'clock call."

Pellegrino paced to Jason's end of the table. "Maybe this will help. As a security measure, Walter had himself and his family chipped with tracking devices." He pulled up an image on his phone and showed it to Jason. "We tracked Samantha's to a location at a gas station near the Snake River. Discovered the abandoned black van with the tracking chip still inside it." Jason gritted his teeth against the picture of a plastic bag holding a tiny microchip that still had bits of blood and tissue clinging to it. That must account for the bandage he'd seen on Samantha's shoulder in the video. "A local there said a small group of men with a load of cargo switched vehicles to an all-terrain SUV and four Arctic Cats on a trailer. He didn't get a license plate."

Snowmobiles. Useless in the mud or on paved roads. That many men and equipment like that left tracks. Tracks and high country just tipped the search into Jason's favor. If the tip was legit. "Did this local actually see Samantha? Could be a misdirect to throw off any rescue effort."

Pellegrino pocketed his phone. "He saw crates, rifles, gas cans...and a lumpy, rolled-up rug. Everything else was state of the art. I'm guessing that rug was Samantha."

Jason nodded. Chances were, he was going to come away from this unsanctioned mission with blood on his hands. But saving Samantha Eddington might go a long way toward atoning for the lives he hadn't saved in Kilkut. For Elaine Burkhart's life.

"I'm not a cop," Jason reminded them. He wouldn't be bringing these men in for justice. "If I have to break a few rules to extract your daughter—"

"I have friends in the county sheriff's department," Eddington assured him. "And the lieutenant governor is an old friend from school. If there's any trouble, I'll make sure it goes away."

Jason wasn't sure how much faith he'd put in any of these people. But his decision had been made. He pulled his knit cap over his head. Then he opened the duffel bag and tossed a stack of bills across the table to Marty. "Gas up the chopper. I'll call in once I've secured a rendezvous point. You're flying at first light."

Marty turned his cap around, tugging the bill into place, a sign he meant business. "I'll be ready."

As Marty jogged to the exit, Eddington stood to hand the duffel bag to Jason. "Take it."

"Money isn't what I need. Donate it to a veterans' charity and survivors' scholarship fund."

"Done." Walter extended a hand. After a moment, Jason reached out to take it. He was surprised to feel the older man transfer the chain and locket he'd been holding into the palm of his hand. "So she'll trust you. Bring my daughter home."

With a sharp nod, Jason pocketed the necklace and strode out the door, heading to his gray 4x4 pickup. The rain limited his scan for activity up and down the street. He wasn't surprised to see that Junior and his crew had driven off in their trucks and SUVs. He *was* surprised that there was no sign of Metz or Grazer. Had they ducked behind the tinted windows of the Eddington limo to avoid the elements? For two men so interested in Samantha Eddington's well-being—or maybe just their standing with the family—they hadn't waited around to find out if he'd agreed to Eddington's rescue request. Unless one or both men had gone off on some fool's errand to track down Samantha himself. Jason paused with a hand on the scratched-up paint of the truck's door handle. A wildcard like a guilt-ridden fiancé or eager-to-please bodyguard could be problematic to the speed and focus of his mission tonight.

And his focus was already compromised. He might be dealing with snow instead of sand, freezing nights versus mind-cooking heat—but the resolve to complete this mission was the same. He'd failed Elaine.

He squeezed his eyes shut as if that could blank the memory of the embedded reporter his unit had been sent to rescue. He and Elaine had spent a lot of late nights together, talking about work at first, then home and hopes and how crazy it was that they should find each other and fall in love over in the

Heat Locker. Yeah, she'd talked about her affair with her bureau chief back in Stuttgart, and how she ought to feel guilty for getting close to one of the jarheads in the unit she was covering. But for those few weeks they'd been together, those precious nights they'd shared, the world and the war hadn't mattered. If she hadn't been so dedicated to putting her job first, she wouldn't have been taken. If he hadn't waited for orders to come through before going after her…

"Mr. Hunt? Hold up." Jason shook off the painful memories, turning to see Dante Pellegrino jog across the street. "Metz isn't the only one who wants to help make this rescue happen. It's my job to protect this family. I started this security firm on my own dime. The reputation of my company is at stake here. It'll put me out of business if we lose Eddington's daughter, and I can't afford that." If Pellegrino was as good as he claimed, Samantha Eddington wouldn't have been kidnapped in the first place. "What do you need from me and my crew?"

"Nothing." Jason wasn't about to trust anyone's chain of command but his own. He didn't care about Pellegrino's reputation or the financial solvency of his business. All he cared about was a frightened woman with glasses, and putting old nightmares to rest. "The fewer people I'm responsible for, the faster I can move."

"You don't want any backup? Weapons? Night-vision goggles? A newer truck to tackle those roads?"

Jason reached into the bed of his truck and picked up one of the logs he stored there to add weight and give the back axle more traction. "This baby's gotten me through plenty of bad weather and rough terrain."

Pellegrino thumbed over his shoulder toward the bar, indicating the patrons inside. "You can talk miracle rescues all you want in front of those civilians. But I know the risk you're taking. You're going up against dangerous men who don't care who gets hurt." Jason watched the drops of rain beading on that ridiculous mustache. "There were at least five men involved in Brandon's attack and the kidnapping. Probably more. The second they hear your approach, you'll be a dead man."

Jason tossed the log into the back of the truck and opened the truck door. "They won't hear me."

"No one expects you to go up against those kinds of odds alone. Let us be part of your team. My men are trained to deal with mercenaries like this."

Jason climbed up behind the wheel. "They're not trained to deal with that mountain. It'll be the only ally I need."

Chapter Four

"Mama?"

Samantha's shivering and her empty belly filled her sleep with familiar dreams. The sedative working its way through her system morphed those dreams into nightmares.

"Mama, where are you?" She was a little girl again, searching through every room of the house for her mother, smelling her sweet perfume, wondering why she wasn't coming upstairs to read her a story and tuck her in. All the rooms were dark, every door locked. She heard thumps and footfalls and angry growls from shadowy corners, but she couldn't see the monsters lurking there. She only knew the monsters were real, lying in wait for a little girl who was all alone.

The house was so cold. Her long hair hardened into shards of ice that poked her neck and shoulders. Her glasses fogged over, and she could barely see. She rattled every doorknob, pounded on wood that wouldn't budge. She fled from one closed room to another, scratching her way through locks and doors until her hands bled. She threw herself against every barrier, breaking through only to find more darkness. She felt the cold, fetid breath of the monsters as they stirred from the shadows and pursued her.

"Stay away," she murmured.

She always slept deeply, securely, when her mother sat on the bed beside her, reading until Samantha's eyes grew heavy and her head tumbled onto her pillow. But tonight, she was running, searching, panicked, bleeding. "Mama?"

She couldn't sleep. She wanted a story. She wanted to melt into the warmth and softness of her mother's body next to hers. She wanted to hear that gently articulate voice in her ears, filling up her head with magic and science, imaginary worlds and characters whose ideas and adventures Samantha wanted to be part of one day.

But she couldn't find her mother. Her tears had frozen on her cheeks. Her pajamas itched against her skin, and every desperate step she took hurt. She was trapped in the darkness. Trapped with monsters, alone and afraid. A cold hand closed around her arm, but she shook it off. Ran. "I can't find you, Mama. Help me."

And then she found a door with light blazing outward from every crack around it. Someone was awake. Someone was alive. She wasn't alone.

"Mama!" Samantha ran, raw nerves stabbing her frozen feet with every step. But hands reached for her from the shadows. Fingers, gnarled like tree limbs, crawled against her skin and tangled in her broken hair. Large hands, strong and unforgiving, closed around her arms and dragged her back into the darkness. "No!"

She fought against the hands. Shoved. Twisted.

The darkness exploded with a loud crash and Samantha screamed. Only the sound stopped up her ears and rang against her skull. She fought to get to the light. Fought to get to her mother. To warmth. To safety.

The shadows closed in all around her, suffocated her. The terrible hands pulled her down, down, snatching at her, grasping her, burying her in the darkness.

"Mama!" she cried out, the timbre of her voice sounding wrong. Older. Deeper. Hoarser.

"Quiet." Not a sound of comfort. Something deeper. More dangerous. A warning.

Too many hands, reaching, grabbing, wanting a piece of a little girl who'd already lost the most precious thing in her life.

False hands, pretending to love her, but offering pain and betrayal, using her.

Rough hands, lifting her off her feet, pushing her inside a van, stealing her ability to see. Hands that didn't care if she was hurt or cold or tired or afraid. Too many hands.

Samantha squirmed and twisted and kicked against the nightmare.

The monster cursed.

"Damn it, woman. I'm not hurting you."

She fought through the dark fog of her brain. She

fought for her mama, fought for her freedom. Fought against her kidnappers.

She was trapped, pinned beneath the heavy weight of all that she had lost, of everything she feared, everything that controlled her. Samantha battled the hands in her dream, wrestling with monsters as she came awake, screaming.

Her eyes opened to the reality of two granite-colored eyes inches above her face, eyes that seemed to capture the haze of moonlight reflecting off the snow outside and glow in the dusty air of the cabin. Such mysterious, masculine eyes.

A man was on top of her. A very large man, with shoulders that filled up the limits of her vision, and hips that pinned her to the floor in the most intimate of positions. A long, muscular thigh was wedged between hers, and something cold and hard poked against her hip. Her arms were splayed over her head on the twisted rag rug where she must have struggled with him. He needed only one hand to pin her cinched-up wrists in place. The other hand had a hard grip on her mouth, cheeks and jaw, absorbing every sound she made. He used the rest of his body to keep her still. It was an effective tool. His chest was as solid and unforgiving as the thick wood planks of the cabin floor.

Her nostrils flared with shock, but her lungs refused to expand. What was happening? Was she still dreaming? Was this a side effect of the drug-induced sleep she'd slipped in and out of for the past several hours?

One of the monsters from her nightmare had caught her.

Samantha squeezed her eyes shut, then blinked them open again. He was still there. This monster was real, pinning her to the floor, his warm breath brushing across her cheek. Clarity rushed in along with fear and the awareness of just how completely vulnerable she was, crushed beneath the weight of the big man's body. His muscular thigh pressed with humiliating familiarity against the most feminine part of her, igniting sensations she didn't want to feel.

Don't hurt me. Please don't hurt me. She tried to speak, but her mouth and jaw were anchored shut by his hard, leather-gloved hand.

Was this some new torture her kidnappers were playing on her? Was rape now on the list of assaults that included threats, guns and drugs?

Only, her kidnappers didn't have faces. They all wore masks. And this man very definitely had a face. Not a handsome one. But taut, compelling, dangerous. Even the dusting of a dark brown beard across his jaw and neck didn't soften the rugged contours of the facade that could have been carved from the same granite that colored his eyes.

A grizzly bear of a man.

"You're awake. No more kicking. And do not scream again," he warned. Her kidnappers didn't have hushed, deep-pitched voices that vibrated from their chests into hers, either.

Samantha nodded her compliance, inhaling a shallow breath as he removed his hand and propped it on

the braided rug beside her head. When he released
her arms, she pulled her hands beneath her chin,
trying to wedge some space between her body and
his. The fact that his hips and chest still pressed into
hers indicated that he didn't entirely trust her. *The
feeling is mutual, buddy.*

"Samantha Eddington?"

She nodded again.

"You hurt? Concussion? Broken bones? Internal
injuries?"

She tapped her fingers against the sandpapery
stubble of beard that darkened his chin, the only
part of him she could reach in this position. "Can't
breathe."

He did a push-up, shifting his weight off her, and
she sucked in a much-needed breath of air, filling
her nose with the scents of pine and cold coming off
his clothes and skin. "Scrapes and bruises as far as
I can tell." Her voice came out in a crackly rasp. "A
little dizzy from the sedatives. Sore throat."

In a surprisingly graceful movement for such a
large man, he grasped the hand she'd touched him
with and helped her sit up as he shoved aside a limp
body that lay on the rug beside her.

A body?

The moment he released her, Samantha scooted
away on her bottom, retreating until her back hit the
log-and-plaster wall. Whether she was fleeing him
or the lump of man at her feet, though, she wasn't
sure. She dragged her knees up to her chest, making sure her bare toes didn't touch the lifeless man.

"Who are you? Is he dead? Did you kill him? Did you kill the other guard? There were two of them." But she couldn't hear either one of them now. A chill of absolute panic shivered across her skin, despite the lightweight coat that covered her arms. Had she just switched one kind of terror for something new? Where had this mountain man come from, and what did he want with her? "Are you going to kill *me*?"

"No," he answered, tucking a gag into the limp man's mouth and dragging him into the shadows beyond her line of sight.

The kidnappers must not be dead. There'd be no reason to muzzle a dead man. A knocker-outer was better than waking up to a murderer lying on top of her. Good.

Samantha shook her head, clearing her wandering thoughts. There was nothing good about her situation. She'd been bound and drugged and held hostage in the rickety old cabin in the wilderness somewhere up above Teton Canyon. She was freezing, hungry. And now a new threat had entered the cabin and crushed her beneath every inch of his hard, muscular body.

Why was it so dark in here? The men who'd stayed with her this time had been playing poker on the chipped enamel kitchen table, with a battery-powered lantern illuminating their cards. There was no lantern now, only the glow of the small heating stove that barely reached her corner, and the moonlight streaming in through the window. Samantha hugged her bound arms around her legs, unable to decide which was more frightening—having the big scary man in her face where she could see him, or knowing he was lurking somewhere in the darkness around her. "What do you want from me?" Her throat was raw from too much screaming and trying to reason with unreasonable men. She coughed, swallowed against the irritated rasp of her throat and spoke again. "Who are you?"

His deep voice was an ominous growl from the blur of shadows. "I'm not one of them."

"And I'm just supposed to believe that?" Fear and confusion still rattled around her brain. "They leave two men with me all the time, but they've changed shifts three times, so there are at least six of them. These two aren't the ones who took me from the lodge, so that makes a minimum of seven. I can tell because their body shapes and voices are different. There's the bully with the gun and the slimy one with all the lewd comments who thinks he's funny and the little guy who compensates by being extra physical." Samantha gently prodded the bruises on her knees. When her numb feet hadn't been able to keep up with the brisk walk from the SUV to the cabin's front door, he'd dragged her up the porch steps. "They go on patrols outside. They talk about sleeping in the truck because it's warmer. And there's some guy named Buck they keep saying has called, or they need to call, or he's coming here, or..." Lord, she was rattling on like a crazy woman. She pressed her parched lips together to stop the flow of words long enough to make her point. "Are you Buck? Are you the man they answer to?"

She heard a groan from the darkness and soft ratcheting noises she could now identify as the sound of zip ties binding someone into place. She looked at the raw skin beneath the plastic tying her wrists together, but quickly glanced up when the man re-emerged from the shadows. A flitting image from her nightmare dissipated with the click of a flash-light. The small beam of light brought hope to her world as he knelt beside her. He unzipped a pocket in his dark gray cargo pants and pulled out a silver chain. "I don't know who Buck is. I don't know who either of these two men are, or the guy in the SUV out front. I'm Captain Jason Hunt. United States Marines. I'm one of the good guys."

Leave it to her father to hire the Marines to come after her. She squinted the coffee-colored hair hanging over his collar into focus. "You don't look like a Marine."

His grim expression turned grimmer. "*Former* Marine. I work search and rescue now."

"Oh." Recognizing the engraved locket he dangled from the end of the chain, Samantha snatched the necklace from his hand. "This was my mother's. Where did you get it?"

"A token from your father. He sent me to find you and bring you home. Said you'd understand why he wasn't paying to get you back."

She ran her thumb over the initials *ME* and *WE* etched into the sterling silver, then opened the latch to study the faded images of her parents, taking comfort in the item that had been so precious to her mother, and therefore to Samantha and her father. Remembrance and relief surged through her system with such force that tears stung her eyes. "I do."

"I need you to do exactly as I say. And no crying. You'll dehydrate." What the man lacked in reassuring comfort, he made up for in concise practicality. He handed her a water bottle from the backpack looped over his shoulders. "Drink."

After swiping at the tears trailing down her cheeks, she opened the bottle and took several long swallows. Feeling slightly better after having addressed that basic need, Samantha dredged up a smile of gratitude for her rescuer. But he was no longer there to see it. Captain Jason Hunt knew her father. Jason Hunt was here to get her out of this nightmare. Jason Hunt had found her in a remote cabin on the western edge of the Tetons and single-handedly subdued two of her kidnappers. Possibly three, if the man who'd talked about sleeping in the truck was still out there. And now she was alone with him.

Was the man with ghostly gray eyes supposed to make her feel safe? She listened to him prowl about the cabin, cracking open the front door to check outside, rifling through the kidnappers' supplies, disabling what she assumed were weapons and opening the back window to a rush of frigid air to toss small boxes—ammunition perhaps?—into the snow. Her smile faded, and she rubbed at the familiar itch on her torso. Since she was clearly no great judge of whom she should trust, Samantha would be smart to adopt the same wary urgency radiating off her self-proclaimed savior. "Do you work for Mr. Pellegrino? He's former military, too."

"I met him."

Was that a yes or a no? Did that make him a bodyguard? Samantha took another drink. He certainly wasn't much of a conversationalist. Kyle had always been able to fill up the awkward silence of a room and put her at ease when her mouth couldn't keep up with all the thoughts pinging through her brain and she just shut down. Only now she realized Kyle had been nothing but talk—greedy, self-serving, tell-Samantha-whatever-she-needs-to-hear talk. Her heart pinched with the ache of losing the man she'd thought she loved. Or maybe that was her ego, as bruised and tender as the rest of her body from the discovery that she'd been a naive fool.

This man was nothing like Kyle. He was bigger. Rawer. Less about charm and more about efficiency. Was he a cop? FBI? A mercenary her father had hired? Some backwoods mountain man Dante Pellegrino had unearthed to find her? Bearing so little resemblance to her would-be fiancé should be a good thing, right? Maybe Jason Hunt had brought someone else with him who could make her feel a little surer about trusting him. "What's next? Are the rest of your men waiting outside?"

Instead of answering, he knelt in front of her

again, holding out a real gift. "I took these off the guy by the door. Didn't look like his style."

"Thank you!" Samantha set down the water bottle to take her glasses from his hand. She hugged them to her chest for a brief, grateful moment before putting them on. "I've been so blind. At such a disadvantage. What…?"

Just as his face and the black knit cap he wore came into focus, he pulled a knife as big as her forearm from his belt. When she shied away from the vicious blade, he grabbed her wrists, pulling her toward him as he sliced through the plastic bindings. Her startled breath returned as slowly as the feeling seeping back into her extremities. "Flex your fingers and toes. Get the circulation going again. Put your shoes on and let's get out of here before the others get back."

"Um…" She picked up what remained of one of her patent-leather shoes. The short, overcompensation guy with a temper had broken off the heel and thrown it at her after she'd gouged a chunk of skin out of his leg during a failed attempt to run away when he'd taken her to use the outhouse behind the cabin. "I didn't exactly have time to pack a change of clothes."

Jason cursed at the shoe that had proved useless in the snow outside, even if it hadn't been snapped in two. "How much do you weigh? I'll carry you." He doused the flashlight and started adjusting his gear around his waist and back. He unhooked his pack and tossed her a pair of thick wool socks. "Put those on. If we can keep your feet dry, there's a chance you won't get frostbite before sunrise."

"There's no one else but you?" She suspected his lack of an answer was her answer. Just the two of them. She nodded her understanding, although she couldn't stop her mind from calculating the odds that were not in their favor. With her glasses giving her twenty/twenty vision again, her eyes quickly adjusted to the dusky cabin to get a clearer look at her surroundings. Yes, Jason Hunt certainly looked fit and capable. He seemed to be nothing but muscle and hard angles and a dangerous, coiled energy. And there was no mistaking the threat of the gun holstered around his thigh or the way he'd handled that hunting knife. But the threat from her kidnappers was very real. And they were outnumbered. "How far away is your vehicle?" No answer. "Skis? Dog sled?"

"Socks." He nodded to her icy toes. Again, no answer. Just a new command. "We need to walk about five miles to get to a buddy of mine with a helicopter. He'll fly us out of here. On your feet."

Five miles? No one was carrying her that far. Hadn't she been manhandled enough over the past several hours? Besides, she was tired of feeling helpless. Done with feeling like she was a burden that had to be dealt with. Samantha pulled on the socks that came up to her knees and tried to get up, fighting off a wave of nausea as the remnants of the sedative in her system spun the room around her. When the vertigo passed, she gritted her teeth against the subsequent headache that throbbed against her skull and braced her hand against the rough log wall. "Can't we steal their truck?"

"It can't handle the terrain we've got to cover."

Clinging to the wall, Samantha pushed to her feet. No dizziness. Good. But she was far from ready to hike five miles across a mountain. "One of their snowmobiles? I saw four."

"Gone." Snap. Click. He'd lightened his pack by tucking several items into the pockets of his cargo pants and insulated jacket.

"They'll be back. All of them. They said they had another tape they needed me to record before sending it at eight in the morning. They complained about not having any cell service up here, so they must go somewhere else to send it to Dad. What time is it?" She moved away from the wall, testing her ability to walk. The warmth of the socks pierced the numbness of cold and inactivity, shooting tiny sparks through her feet. But the pain shocked the last of the fatigue out of her system. "They're not out patrolling the area?"

"Now that the storm has passed, it's a clear night. We'd hear the noise of the engines if they were close by." Something buzzed on Jason's wrist, and he pulled back his sleeve to turn off the alarm on his watch. "Time to go. Ready?"

One of the men lying near the door groaned. Although they'd been gagged and hog-tied, and Jason had taken their weapons, the kidnapper was stirring. *Stirring* couldn't be good for a successful getaway.

Samantha's brain suddenly kicked into a higher gear. Why hadn't she thought of this sooner? She looped the chain around her neck and kissed the locket before stuffing it inside the neckline of her dress. Hurrying as quickly as the stiffness of her body allowed, she crossed to the metal storage cabinet across the room and pulled it open, blindly feeling around on the top shelf for the items she was far too familiar with. Her fingers closed around a small glass vial. "Are they waking up?"

"We won't be here to find out. What are you doing?"

"Buying us more time to get away." She pulled down a syringe packet and tore off the paper, measuring out a dose of the sedative the kidnappers had used on her. She injected Moaning Man, checking his pulse after he quieted. Breathing, but asleep. Then she opened a new packet and injected the second man. "Buying me enough time to do this."

She measured the size of her foot against both men, then sat down beside the one with the smaller boots and started untying them.

Jason's sigh was as impatient as the brisk wind outside the cabin. Still, he surprised her by kneeling beside her and picking up the other boot to loosen the laces. "If these are too big, they'll rub blisters. Then I'll definitely be carrying you."

"I think I'll be okay with these thick socks. A few minutes now will save us time later. You can move faster if you're not hauling me on your back, right?"

She held his gaze until he gave her a sharp nod.

"I so wish I had a pair of pants or long johns." She

pulled off the first boot and lifted the black camo canvas of the guy's pant leg. "You don't suppose—"

Jason grabbed her wrist and shoved the second boot into her hand, ending her search. "It's not that far, and the sun will be up in another hour. Move it, Princess."

Princess? Samantha bristled at the tossed-off nickname. Sure. The party dress and ridiculous heels? A $5 million bargaining chip? He probably had her pegged as one of the society princesses her father and stepmother so desperately wanted her to be. If only he knew.

But he didn't give her time to take offense or correct his impression of her. He pulled the black knit stocking masks off the unconscious men. "You recognize either of them?" he asked.

She spared a quick glance for the two men, a bald one with bruising around the tattoos on his throat and the other with blood matted in the hair at his temple. Strangers. Two men she'd never laid eyes on before who'd hurt her and promised more than once to kill her if she didn't cooperate. Samantha went back to securing the second boot. "No. Should I?"

"They've got fighting skills, sophisticated weaponry…" He picked up one of the syringes she'd discarded and tossed it into the darkness. "…access to drugs. Enough players involved to rotate shifts and carry out different assignments."

"Meaning?"

"Meaning these guys aren't amateurs. Your father said he doesn't care who's responsible as long as my mission is a success. But it would have been nice to know exactly what I was up against."

"Mission?" Samantha tied a second knot to keep the boot secure around her ankle. She looked at her abductors with fresh eyes. Matching black camo outfits. The arsenal of rifles and guns she'd seen. "Are they military?"

The whiny buzz of a distant engine pierced the night. Make that two engines. More than two. She recognized the sound. Snowmobiles. Her captors were returning.

She'd barely acknowledged the terror that suddenly immobilized her when Jason lifted her right off the floor, setting her on her feet beside him just inside the door as he opened it a little wider to peer into the milky darkness outside the cabin. "You *can* hear them," she whispered. Like mutant hornets swarming through the trees. Samantha pushed Jason toward the door. Well, *pushed* was a relative term. She pushed, and he didn't budge. But she was about to be trapped in this cabin. Again. "How far do you think—?"

Jason clamped his hand over her mouth again, tilting her face up to his. Right. That glare meant *shut up, Princess*.

Those mysterious eyes, framed by lines of sun and outdoor living, held hers a moment longer until she nodded. He released her and dropped down to check the fit of her boots, his big hands easily spanning, squeezing, adjusting. On the way back up, he tied the belt of her black-and-white coat, cinching it snugly around her waist. He towered above her for a moment, assessing either side of her face. Before she could question his perusal and what he found off-putting enough to make him grimace like that, he pulled a knit cap off the bald man and plopped it on top of her head, stretching it over pins and tangles until her ears were covered.

Then he turned to the opening and held up his fist. "This means stop. Talking, moving, whatever. I don't care how scared you are, listen to what I say and do what I tell you. Your life may depend on it." He unholstered his gun and gripped it in his right hand, reaching back with his left to pull her onto the porch behind him. The noise of the gunning engines seemed to bounce off every hard surface around her—the cabin door she pulled shut, the forest of trees surrounding the perimeter of the clearing, the cliff wall on the far side of the gravel road and the rocky outcropping just a few yards beyond the edge of the porch—making it impossible for her to tell how far away her abductors were, or even from which direction they were coming. "Walk where I walk. I've already made a couple of false trails in the snow to keep them busy and force them to split up. Move as quickly as you can. Don't say a word."

He stepped off the porch, expecting her to follow. Sinking up to her ankles in the trampled slush and fresh layer of snow, she was glad she'd thought to steal the pair of boots to protect her feet and at least give her a chance at staying warm. "Did my father really send you? Or am I walking off into the wilderness with a stranger, never to be seen again?"

Her head was down, watching each slippery step, when she bumped into his backpack.

Jason had stopped abruptly. He inhaled a deep breath before he pushed her into the shadows at the side of the cabin and hunched down to level his gaze with hers. "I have three rules. Do what I tell you. Don't get wet. And do what I tell you."

"That's only two. Is the fist thing the third rule—?"

He plastered his hand over her mouth again. "Noise carries in this cold air. Those men have friends who will kill us if they find us. They will find us if they hear you. Understand?"

That seemed clear enough. A cloud of his warm breath fogged her glasses, forcing her to tilt her eyes above the rims to see the warning stamped on his hard expression.

"I know you're not used to situations like this. But I am. Let me do my job. I will keep you safe. I won't let these men hurt you again." Was he trying to tell her she didn't need to be afraid with him around? That she needed to trust him? Maybe she'd be safe from the bad guys, but Jason Hunt's size and strength, his terse commands and grabby hands, not to mention the knife and the gun, still made her very nervous. "Keep up. Remember the rules. And I'll make sure you get home to Daddy."

That reassurance would have to do for now. Samantha nodded one more time before he released her. He peeked around the cabin, checking the man sleeping in the truck, evaluating the distance and arrival time of the approaching snowmobiles. This time, when he stepped out, he moved at a quicker pace, forcing Samantha into a jog to stay close behind him.

As the echoing drone of the snowmobiles closed in around them, Jason entered the tree line, moving with unerring speed through the obstacles of pines and terrain. Samantha plunged into the woods behind him—following Jason's broad back into the cold, moonlit night, leaving shelter, her kidnappers and the luxury of doubting this man behind.

Chapter Five

He was a mile and a half from redemption.

Jason climbed on top of the thick lodgepole pine that had been toppled by a forest fire years earlier. Now, the charred trunk gave moss and lichens a place to grow and provided shelter for the squirrel that scurried from beneath it and raced up a neighboring snag, or dead tree that was still standing upright. He watched the little critter leave its tiny tracks in the snow, and instinctively glanced over his shoulder to make sure Sam was still following in his footsteps about twenty yards behind him. He'd led her on a path close to the trunks where the snow wasn't as deep and was already disturbed by animals, drifts, and snow melting and dropping from higher up in the trees, making their boot prints harder to follow.

But he'd pushed the pace to reach the rendezvous point at Mule Deer Pass by 8:00 a.m., and she was getting tired, based on puffs of breath clouding around her face in the cold air. A short break would do her good. Allowing himself a moment to rest as well, he tilted his face to the pink and gold rays of morning sun that pierced the canopy of dark green branches above him. The stars had long been swallowed up with the grayish haze of dawn. And though the sun had barely crested the tree line of the lower elevations off to the east, Jason could feel the promise of a new day coursing through him—knowing that he was close to completing this mission without a single casualty. He hadn't failed. He'd made a quick hike with a light pack up the crest trail toward Teton Canyon between the south and middle peaks, taking a shortcut to the line of supply shacks that fit the clues from Sam's video and the intel Dante Pellegrino and his man had given him.

The burn in his thigh and calf muscles and the dampness of the brisk morning breeze cooling the skin around his cheeks created a yin and yang of sensations inside him that made him feel alive. Useful. Living squarely in the present. He inhaled a cool, fresh breath that filled his lungs and eased the tightness of guilt and regret he normally carried with him. They weren't out of the woods yet, literally or figuratively, but redemption felt pretty damn good.

His long strides feeling lighter now, Jason stepped down and made a quick visual sweep through the trees in every direction. Not that he'd heard, seen or sensed anyone closing in on their trail.

So far, this op had gone pretty much according to plan. He'd spotted the man sleeping in the truck with the trailer hitch outside the second cabin. It had been easy to surprise him and subdue him with a choke hold before the guy even had a chance to cry out or

alert his buddies. The two men inside had been arguing loudly enough over why they'd drawn the short
straw and hadn't been able to go down into town with
the others that Jason had scouted out the cabin and
kicked in the front door before either of them had a
chance to draw their weapons. Stooge One had gone
down with a blow to the head while his buddy had
required a few seconds of hand-to-hand combat before he'd succumbed to Jason's forearm cutting off
the flow of oxygen to his brain.

Sam herself had been a little trickier to subdue.
He'd needed her to wake up, so she wouldn't startle
and alert anyone within hearing range of his presence. A gun butt to the temple or a choke hold around
the neck had been out of the question, but she'd come
out of her drugged-up sleep disoriented and violent.
He had the bruise on his inner thigh, a little too
close to the family jewels for his liking, from the
kick that had connected before he realized that a
friendly nudge awake wasn't going to work. He'd
pinned her flailing limbs the best way he knew how
without hurting her, and had wound up frightening
her even more when she'd come to and found him
lying on top of her. The frankly sexual position had
achieved his goal of securing each limb so that she
couldn't strike him again. But those few seconds of
having a soft, curvy woman stretched out beneath
him had done something to him, too.

His toe caught a rock and he nearly stumbled
at the distracting memory of generous breasts and
earth-mother hips plastered against his harder frame.

Jason shook off the answering surge of base male awareness that heated his blood and made sure he was centered over his feet again. No matter how long he'd been without female companionship, no matter how long it had been since he'd even hit on a lady, Sam Eddington was a mission objective, not a uniquely attractive woman.

And until he delivered her safely into the arms of her father, he'd do well to remember that.

With a resolute breath, he checked his watch and the attached compass for both time and direction, confirming what the angle of the sun and the years he'd spent hiking these mountains had already told him. Marty should already be en route to their destination, and within the hour, they'd be landing at the airstrip outside Jackson. The bad guys had taken the bait and split up to follow the false trails he'd left along the service road and down the mountain in the opposite direction. Both were easier paths than the steeper route he was taking south to the high-altitude clearing of Mule Deer Pass. Even if they did find the right trail, the snowmobiles would be the only vehicle that could handle the rough terrain. With all these trees, they wouldn't be able to go full throttle. Plus, there would be no way to mask their approach, giving Jason plenty of time to hide Sam and backtrack along the rocky incline to deal with them if he had to.

But if his luck held, he wouldn't have to deal with anyone but the woman behind him. He pulled his bottle of water and drank a couple of long swallows before attaching it back to his pack. "About three clicks away now, Princess."

The grunt behind him sounded a little different this time, more of a groan of irritation than the slightly winded sound of determination he'd been listening to for the past three miles. "I resent that, you know."

Jason turned to see Sam sit on the far side of the fallen tree trunk, pausing a moment to inhale a deep breath before swinging her leg over the top. Her checkered coat and frilly dress rode up past the edge of the skin-colored underwear that clung to her thighs, and he caught a glimpse of long, strong legs as she plopped into the snow on the other side. At least she was getting one rule right—she followed in his steps, plunging into the snow where it was deeper, and shuffling along a little faster where wind or the dense canopy of overhanging pine boughs had cleared the exposed rocks and hard-packed dirt. As for staying quiet...?

"My feet are doing okay, but I can hardly feel the skin on my legs anymore. Pink skin means they're getting chapped, right?" She tugged her clothes back into place and leaned back against the tree trunk. "I wore this dress for press photographers, not trekking through the mountains. What I wouldn't give for long pants. Or an electric blanket."

"The hike will be over soon," he assured her. "A click is only—"

"A thousand meters. A kilometer. I know. It's about the distance between each line or click on a

rifle scope when you're sighting a target." That was
an odd chunk of information to have stored away in
that blond head of hers. But her father had said she
knew her way around guns. "What I resent is the
nickname. Princess. I find that offensive. I don't call
you Mountain Man or Big Scary Dude, do I?" Was
that how she saw him? He supposed the descriptors
fit. And he hadn't exactly given her reason to see him
any other way. "You don't even know me. It sounds
derisive, like you don't respect me, or you don't respect people *like* me. Oh." Sam quieted, pulling out
the water bottle he'd given her and taking a sip. Although he suspected the pause had more to do with
catching her breath, Jason gave her a once-over to
make sure he wasn't pushing her too hard and she
could finish the hike. "I fit the stereotype, don't I?"

"Stereotype?" He caught her hands between his
as she rubbed them together.

"Poor little rich girl? All dolled up and dumb
enough to get herself kidnapped?" Jason tugged his
gloves off with his teeth to feel the temperature of
her skin. Her fingers had been pink the last time
he'd checked how she was handling exposure to the
elements. Now, even with massaging them between
his palms, they were stiff and pale. "I have two college degrees. But I guess being book smart doesn't
make me smart about people. You know who I was
running away from last night? The man my father
and stepmother handpicked for me to marry. Ooh.
I hear it now. Having a *handpicked* boyfriend does
make me sound a little like a princess." She winced

as he pressed her fingers between his. Or maybe that was the face she made when she realized she was revealing more than she wanted. "I knew something wasn't right between us, but I didn't trust my gut. I found Kyle in the closet with my sister. And they weren't picking out clothes." She tugged her hands from his, and he glanced up to see her eyes widen behind her glasses. "Sorry. That's too much information, isn't it?"

That revelation explained a lot about Kyle Grazer's and Taylor Eddington's behavior last night at Kitty's Bar. If he knew nothing else about Sam Eddington, Jason knew the woman had courage. She'd done what she could to help herself get rescued, even with a gun pointed at her head. She'd kept up with him on this fast trek to freedom. And she'd had the sense to walk away from the selfish hothead he'd met last night. Curvy body. Pretty eyes. A brave heart. There was a lot to admire about...

Mission. Objective. Jason lectured himself silently, halting any thoughts of attraction. Saving Elaine from the insurgents who'd kidnapped her in Kilkut had been all too personal—and she'd died. He needed to keep this relationship distant and professional, or the mistakes that haunted him could become all too real again.

Besides, this mission would be over in about sixty minutes. Hardly enough time to even think the word *relationship*, much less contemplate getting involved with a woman with whom he had so little in common.

He tugged one of the gloves from his teeth and

slipped it onto her right hand. "Your legs will survive because there's meat on them. I'm more worried about your extremities." He slipped the second glove into place, carefully avoiding the abrasions around her wrists. "We should have grabbed a pair off one of the men in the cabin. Better?"

"Better. What about your hands?"

"I'm tougher than you are. Bigger. More body heat. Feet?" Jason knelt in front of her to check her boots. He slipped his finger inside and ran it around her ankle, ensuring her socks were dry.

"Aching." She wiggled her toes against the squeeze of his hands, reassuring him that she wasn't suffering from frostbite.

"Blisters?"

"Not that I can tell."

"That was a good call to take these."

"Thank you."

He patted her knee before pushing to his feet. "Let's keep moving. Your dad is waiting for me to bring you home. I don't want to give those guys a chance to catch up with us."

Jason was already continuing his zigzagging path down the mountain's incline when he heard her fall into step behind him again. "I'll call you Jason or Mr. Hunt. And you can call me Samantha or Miss Eddington, but not Princess. And certainly not baby or Filly One."

"Why would I—?"

"Actually, my full name is Samantha Beryl Geraldine Eddington. I know, it's a mouthful. I'm named after both sets of grandparents. Good thing my last name's Eddington, or there'd probably be an Edwina thrown in there. Sam and Geraldine, Ed and Beryl."

"That's too much to remember." Jason stopped, faced her. He took her hand to help her climb over the next log with a little less effort than the last one before sliding over it himself. He dropped to the ground beside her and kept walking. "How about I call you Sam."

"Beats Princess," she muttered under her breath.

Jason's chest vibrated with a low-pitched chuckle. The woman sure had a lot of words in her. They didn't all make sense when she rattled on like this. But every now and then, her sarcasm made him want to laugh.

Smaller trees that indicated newer forest growth, and the mounds of detritus that had rolled down from a rockslide higher up the mountain, told Jason they were nearing the edge of the cliff that would curve around a deep washout to take them to their destination. He nodded to a small boulder where Sam could rest while he pulled the two-way radio from his pack to call Marty Flynn and confirm his ETA at the extraction point.

"Sierra Romeo Seven One Five, this is Ground Team One. Come in. Sierra Romeo Seven One Five, this is Ground Team One. What's your twenty? Over." The crackle of static was his only response to his request for Marty's location. Jason paused to look up, giving his friend time to answer. Wispy clouds made the sky a pale blue. But even after last night's heavy rain and soft new blanket of snow, the weather was clear enough to fly. "This is Ground Team One. We're approaching the extraction point. Do you copy?" A faint sense of unease narrowed his gaze before he put the radio back to his mouth. "Sierra Romeo Seven One Five, please respond. You'd better not be late, Lieutenant Flynn. Over."

Unwanted voices played in his head.

"We have to wait for air support, Captain!"

"There's no time. Radwan already posted his last broadcast—he's got no reason to keep the hostages alive." Jason unhooked his rifle from his flak vest and readied to make the incursion into Radwan's stronghold. *"I'll go in alone. I can at least scout out which of those blips on the infrared are our hostages, and which are Radwan's men."*

The major shoved Jason back inside the abandoned hut on the edge of Kilkut. "I have my orders, Hunt. Your girlfriend and her cameraman are going to have to wait until I have clearance to send in any men."

"It'll be too late."

"We wait."

"They'll kill her!"

"Is there a problem?"

Jason jerked at the husky voice at his elbow, and pulled himself back into the present. He glanced down at the concerned tilt of Sam's green eyes above the rim of her glasses. He wasn't about to explain where his mind had gone. No sense letting her know that he hadn't saved the last woman he'd gone to res-

cue from kidnappers. And the idea of opening up
and talking about all he had lost and how he should
have been able to change the outcome of that fateful
day grated like a straight-edge razor across his skin.

Without explanation or reassurance, he looked
away from those worried eyes and toggled the call
button on his radio. "Marty? Forget the code talk.
This is Hunt. We're coming up on Mule Deer Pass.
Are you reading me? Over."

The crackle of static was the only response he
got on either of the frequencies he tried. Since he
couldn't hear the telltale whup-whup of helicopter
blades in the air, either his red-haired buddy was running behind schedule, or Marty had already landed
the chopper. If that was the case, though, he would
be in range of Jason's radio signal and he should answer. Clipping the radio back onto his pack, Jason
climbed out to the rim of the drop-off and searched
the sky and the surrounding gorge. If Marty wasn't
in range, that meant there'd been a problem of some
kind. Weather at a lower altitude. Mechanical issue.
Trouble getting his flight plan cleared.

Jason studied the familiar terrain, evaluating his
options. Any delay meant he and Sam would be alone
on the mountain longer than planned. Delays meant
more time for her kidnappers to come to, gather their
full numbers—however many that was—and catch
up with them.

He had a really bad feeling about this.

"Your friend's in the Marines, too?" she asked.
"You called him Lieutenant."

"We served together." He closed his eyes and tilted his head, training his ear to the echo of any snowmobiles or hikers in the woods, on the ridge or down in the canyon. Nothing. Save for the wildlife and the wind, the mountains were a naturally quiet place—one of the draws that made this part of the world a sanctuary for him. But this was unnaturally quiet. He opened his eyes, studying the slope above and the drop-off below. "Why aren't we hearing the kidnappers in pursuit?"

"That's a good thing, right? That they haven't found us?"

"You're worth five million dollars to them. Why aren't they coming after you?"

She hugged her arms around her waist. It could be the temperature, but he suspected his words had chilled her. "Because you're really good at what you do?"

If he was really that good, he'd have noticed something was off about this rescue mission earlier. Now he'd noticed. There was no crunch of gravel from vehicles using the service roads, no growl of snowmobiles, no clomp of boots or jangle of gear. He just couldn't put his thumb on what it was he needed to be worried about.

At the very least, Marty's silence was the equivalent of a big red flag. "The pilot's not answering his radio. I'm running ahead to see if I can make visual contact with our ride out of here. Keep a steady pace so you don't get winded. You'll be fine as long as you stay on the trail I make." He grasped her by the shoulders, kneading his fingers into the weather-proofed polyester of her coat and the slim muscles underneath before he backed her several feet away from the rocky overhang and released her. "That drop-off into the gorge is steep. Unless you're half mountain goat, I don't want you tumbling over the edge. Can you remember that while I'm gone?"

She raised her fingers to the edge of her knit cap in a sharp salute. "Yes, sir. Fist means stop. Do what you say. Don't get wet. Don't fall off the mountain."

"And don't call you Princess."

Yeah. Interesting turned pretty when she smiled. "How come my rules outnumber yours? Once I get my hands on a computer or piece of paper, I am so making a list to keep track of them."

But this wasn't the time or place for smiling. He was in trouble already if he was flashing back to Kilkut or thinking she was pretty. This whole op was about getting the job done and easing his conscience. Saving a life in exchange for the one he hadn't. "I'll get you whatever you need once we're off this mountain. Laptop. Pen and paper. Warm clothes."

"A hot shower?"

"Done." He hardened his expression so she'd stop that smiling thing that was getting under his skin and derailing his focus on the mission, then dismissed her with a curt nod. "Stay on my path."

He turned up the mountain and doubled his pace, climbing over rocky crags and around thinning trees until he reached the edge of the relatively flat alpine clearing that had been carved out of the granite eons ago. Relief was far from what he felt when he spotted Marty's red-and-white search and rescue chopper sitting in the middle of the treeless expanse.

"Why didn't you answer me?" he speculated out loud.

Jason paused at the edge of the trees, hanging back in the last bit of cover to assess the situation before he headed out over open ground. Although the rotor was now still, a lot of snow had been stirred up by the chopper blades when Marty had landed, exposing bits of high-mountain grass and glacier lilies peeking up through the ground to reach the sunshine. It was impossible to tell if there were footprints showing he'd left the bird, or that anyone else had approached it. With the tail of the chopper facing him, he couldn't see the cockpit to know if Marty was even on board. Maybe his pal had done something as innocent as walking into the woods to take a leak.

Jason closed his eyes, listening for any sound the young man might make. But the only noises he heard were the crunch of snow beneath boots that were about half the size of his and Sam's openmouthed exhales as she climbed up to the edge of the clearing. "A helicopter. Thank God. I will be so glad to get off this mountain. Is that your friend?"

Jason squeezed his hand into a fist beside his head. Sam stopped behind him, thankfully quiet except for the soft rasps of air as she evened out her breathing.

That is, she was quiet until he unhooked the holster on his thigh and pulled out his Glock. "What's wrong?" Her damaged voice was little more than a husky whisper.

"Something's off. Stay out of sight behind the tree line."

Ten fingers curled around the sleeve of his jacket and nipped into the skin and muscle underneath. "You're coming back, right?"

"That's the idea."

"Good." She tugged against him when he would have gone, and her touch drew his focus down to green eyes that held as much doubt as they did courage. "The last time I put my faith in a man, and he left me...I got kidnapped."

Before he could dismiss the pull he felt toward that brave vulnerability, Jason captured a tendril of toffee-blond hair that had fallen over her cheek and tucked it back beneath the edge of her knit cap, securing it behind her ear. Her eyes widened behind her glasses at the unexpected touch—or maybe that was his own body responding to the sensations of soft, cool skin and silky hair beneath his fingertips. How could a practical gesture feel so much like a caress? Jason curled his fingers into his palm, needing to distance himself from the tender feelings stirring inside him. Emotions had nothing to do with this mission. It was all about saving the girl and reclaiming some measure of solace for his tormented soul—not developing any kind of hormonal attraction or visceral appreciation for said girl. "I'm coming back. As long as you're my responsibility, I'll be close by."

He nudged her toward a trio of scrawny pines and waited for her to hunch down behind them before he moved out. Jason squeezed his gun between both hands, keeping his body low to the ground as if he was clearing a suspected enemy stronghold. His long legs took him quickly to the helicopter, but not only was the mountain unusually quiet, but now his nose could detect a smell in the air that wasn't natural.

He circled around to the front of the chopper, every nerve ending prickling with suspicion when he saw the front door propped open. "Marty? If this is some kind of joke…" He swung his gun around into the opening but lowered it just as quickly. He'd found Marty, all right. "Son of a…"

His lungs burned with a painful breath. The small-bore hole in the side of Marty's red hair, and the spatter of blood on the far seat and window, tried to take him back to Kilkut. But he shoved the memory of all the dead bodies out of his head and lowered his weapon, leaning in to press two fingers to the side of Marty's neck.

Jason swore again. Not only was there no pulse, the pilot's skin was cold to the touch. This hadn't just happened. "Damn it, Marty." He pulled the rim of his friend's blood-soaked ball cap down over his lifeless face. "This was supposed to be easy money for you. Not a death sentence."

So much for doing a friend a favor. So much for redemption.

"Jason? What is it? What's wrong?" He heard

Sam's worried tone a split second before he realized she was out in the open, running toward him.

"What the hell?" Jason met her in two long strides, dragging her in front of him, using the helicopter and his body to shield her from view. "I told you to stay put. You think I want another casualty on my hands?"

"Casualty? Nobody cusses up a blue streak like that unless something really bad... Oh. This *is* really bad." Her back flattened against his chest. Her fingers dug into his forearm still cinched around her waist. "I'm so sorry. This is your friend?"

But Jason was lost in the memories of a war-torn village street where two soldiers and two journalists lay dead among the insurgents who had fallen in the firefight that came too late to save the woman he'd loved. He squeezed his eyes shut against the memory of Elaine's shattered glasses and matted dark hair as he rocked her in his arms. He pulled her tightly to his chest, his hands fisting at the stench of sulfur and smoke filling his head, his whole body clenching with helplessness and guilt and grief. So much blood. So much death. So much loss. It was more than one man could—

"Jason?" The body in his arms pushed against him, wiggling its way into the flashback. That wasn't right. Elaine was dead. No, Marty was the one who'd died. "Jason." A hoarse voice pierced the veil between the present and the past. He inhaled deeply, his lungs filling with cool air. The air in Kilkut burned.

"Hey. You're squeezing the stuffing out of me. Are you okay? He must have been a good friend."

The damn inappropriate reaction to Sam's bottom rubbing against his zipper shocked Jason back to reality. He unlocked the death grip he had around her waist and stepped back, giving her room to turn around. "I'm sorry. I..."

How did he explain how damaged he was? How could he share his guilt with a stranger?

But those green eyes were bright with tears now, as if she understood his pain. And the hands rubbing soothing circles up and down his arms felt familiar. "Tell me about your friend. I know he must have been very brave. He was trying to help me."

Yeah. He was a brave kid, all right. "His name's Marty Flynn. I work with him. *Worked* with him in search and rescue. He's the one who called me last night to help your dad find you. Always such a smooth talker. He was hittin' on your sister. And the waitress. He survived two tours of duty, but not a routine flight into... He was barely old enough to..." He turned his nose to the sky and sucked in another cooling breath before looking down into Sam's caring eyes. "This reminds me of..." No. He didn't want to talk about the past right now. Not with her. He took another breath and centered himself back in the present. "Sorry if I hurt you."

"Your hold wasn't any tighter than this corset thing I'm wearing. I'll live." But for how long if he couldn't keep himself together? She meant to tease a smile out of him, but it wouldn't come. "Do you know how to fly a helicopter?"

A relatively easy search and rescue—for him—just got complicated. Marty Flynn was never going to flirt with a pretty girl or bug him like some sort of adoring puppy dog again. And they weren't flying out of here.

Remember the mission. Think like a Marine. With a sharp nod, Jason slammed the door on his emotions and focused on the job at hand. Step one was recon. Gather intel. Make a plan. "No. I don't suppose you've got a pilot's license?"

She shook her head.

"How'd the kidnappers get here ahead of us?" Jason leaned in beside her to check the helicopter's radio. Marty wasn't the only thing they'd shot up. "We're not calling for backup."

"I slowed you down, didn't I?"

"Not that much. How did they know where the chopper would meet us?"

He pulled back to check the windows and side panel for bullet holes. There were none. The shooter had gotten the drop on Marty the moment he'd opened the door. Or else, Marty had known the shooter and opened the door for him.

He flashed on the memory of a laser-sighted pistol pointed to his chest. A handgun like that could cover almost as much range as a rifle. Whoever shot Marty wouldn't have needed to be that close. But the shooter could certainly be close enough to have them in their sights, too. If he was still nearby.

"They knew we were coming." Instead of following them from the cabin, the kidnappers had gotten out in front of them. But there weren't exactly any road signs indicating the trail Jason had taken to get Sam here. "They knew about Mule Deer Pass."

Beating them to the rendezvous point wasn't the only lucky break the kidnappers had gotten. How had they known when and where she'd be alone so that they could abduct her in the first place?

"You mean Marty told them we were coming here? He's one of *them*?"

Jason drew his weapon again, scanning the landscape beyond the chopper. "He wouldn't do that."

Who all had been in Kitty's Bar last night? Who had Marty talked to between then and now? Who else knew the details of Jason's rescue mission? Who didn't want Samantha Eddington coming home?

Understanding made her skin go pale, and she hugged her arms around her middle. "Are they sending my father a message? Pay up or this is what will happen to me?" Sam straightened under his unblinking scrutiny, then started backing away. "What are you thinking? Damn it, Jase, you're scaring me."

He grabbed her by the shoulders before she retreated beyond arm's reach and pulled her toward the back door of the helicopter. "You afraid of a long walk?"

"No."

"How about a dead body?"

"I don't think so. But I've never seen a guy who's been shot—"

"Close enough." He set her on the running board. "Get inside and stay down. It'll give you a few minutes to warm up while I scope things out."

"You're coming back, right?" she asked, climbing over the seat.

"Get in." He growled at her insecurity, then changed his answer to a succinct "Yes."

Apparently, his word was all the assurance she needed because she spotted something on the floor that caught her interest and she ducked down beneath the dashboard. Good. He had a feeling that out of sight was the best place for Sam to be right now. She was pulling a Mylar blanket from the chopper's medical supplies and covering up Marty when Jason felt it was safe enough to close the door and move away.

Staying close to the helicopter, Jason quickly scanned the top of the ridge. Thanks to glacial ice and rockslides, there was no place for a man to hide up there. Same with the washout downrange of the chopper. But the trees and craggy terrain to either side offered plenty of cover to anyone with a rifle and a steady aim. So where were the kidnappers now? Why hadn't they taken a shot at him yet? If they wanted to recapture Sam for the ransom, they'd have to take him down first.

Why take out the pilot and trap them on the mountain?

His nostrils flared at the pungent odor he'd noticed earlier, and an idea began to take shape. He knelt to swipe his fingers through the snow and soggy grass underneath. Fuel. He visually followed the trail of discolored snow back to the chopper and tracked the oily residue up to the tank near the engine. Marty. The radio. And now the fuel tank—all with nice big bullet holes in them.

A man wouldn't need to shoot them if he could make all their deaths look like an accident. Jason glanced down the incline to see where the fuel had pooled in a snowy depression. This was bad. "Sam?" He pushed to his feet, backing toward the chopper. "Sam?" When he heard rustling in the trees, and spotted at least three upright shadows moving, he ran. This was very bad. He slapped the passenger window. "Sam!"

She popped up, holding a Swiss Army knife in one hand and a backpack in the other as Jason waved her toward the exit. She was stuffing the tool she'd scrounged into the emergency gear bag and hooking it over her shoulder as he slid the door open. "Your friend had a backpack. Warm clothes. A couple of protein bars. Water. Do you think he'd mind if I—"

"We need to go. Now."

She flinched at the crack of a gunshot, tilted her head to the sky as a flare arced like a comet above the clearing. "Is that...?"

Very, very bad. "Run!"

Jason grabbed her around the waist, set her on the ground, snatched her gloved hand and ran back the way they came. The flare hit the fuel, igniting a fire that ran up the slope like a charging bear. He forced Sam into the race of her life as he lengthened his stride and sprinted toward the trees. They'd barely reached the three scrawny pines at the edge of the forest when the helicopter exploded.

Chapter Six

A shock wave of heat knocked them off their feet. Jason hit the ground hard, catching Sam in his arms as they tumbled over and over down the mountain. He felt the bite of every rock, the punch of every root, the rasp of every frightened breath against his neck until he slammed into the trunk of a fallen tree. But there was no time to do anything more than roll Sam beneath him as fire and debris from the chopper rained down from the sky. The bulk of his pack shielded them from most of the shrapnel, but he felt the sharp nick of something hot burning into his left thigh.

Ignoring the pain, he rolled off her, helping her sit up. Her glasses sat cockeyed on her nose, and he pushed them back into place, willing her eyes to focus and tell him she wasn't hurt. She rubbed at the hinge of her jaw, gently shaking her head. "You okay?"

"My ears…" Yeah. His were ringing, too. She eyed her scraped knees and the tear in her coat before catching sight of the blood on his pant leg. "You're hurt."

He batted her hand away when she reached for the singed slice of material. "I'm fine."

For now.

The first thud hit the tree beside them and Jason swore. He lifted her to her feet in front of him as staccato gunshots joined the roar of the burning flames. "Keep moving."

"Are they shooting at us? I'm worth five million dollars to them."

"Into the trees!"

Jason spared a few precious seconds to swing around and return fire.

"He's armed!" someone shouted.

"Son of a…" It looked like half a platoon, all dressed in black camouflage, darting out of the trees on the far side of the clearing. They carried assault rifles and handguns, wore utility vests and stocking masks like the men he'd subdued at the cabin. Their shots were wild right now, with the burning helicopter and the chimeras of rising heat obscuring their sights. But their intention was clear. Eight? Ten men on the hunt? And he and Sam were the prey.

"Move it!" He caught Sam's hand and ran past her, leading her into the shelter of the trees, wondering how long she could keep up this pace at this altitude, evaluating how long it would take the men to get close enough to get an accurate bead on them, worrying about the number of bullets he had left in his sidearm to protect her.

Sam's breathing was labored now, her steps less sure. Jason's brain was in combat mode, but they were outgunned, outmanned. Standing his ground wasn't an option. But maybe he could even up the odds a little bit.

He pulled Sam down behind the tree where they'd stopped earlier. She was breathing way too hard and her skin was far too ashen. "Did I ever tell you...I don't really...work out?" She sucked in another deep breath. "Never been much of a—"

"Don't talk." Jason placed a hand on her shoulder, encouraging her to match the rhythm of his breathing. "Deep breaths. Don't panic."

"I'm going to asphyxiate long before I have the energy to panic."

She covered her ears and sank down as he braced his arms on top of the trunk and aimed the Glock at their pursuers. Now he could hear every damn noise in the book. Snowmobiles. Shouts. Running feet. Who were these guys?

"Circle around!"

"Don't lose them!"

Their point man crested the rise above them. Jason fired. Took him out.

"Jimmy's down!" another man shouted. "Jim—? He's dead! That son of a... They're headed north!"

A second mercenary burst through the tree line, whooping with adrenaline as he unloaded a barrage of automatic gunfire. Jason dived for the ground as the wood splintered and flew around them. More shots shattered branches and kicked up tiny explosions of pine needles, dirt and snow. The wild spray of bullets cut a small tree beside them in half before the gun jammed and the man cursed.

"Jason?" That terrified sound in Sam's crackly voice twisted in his gut. "I'm not afraid to admit that I'm pretty damn scared."

He rose and fired off two more shots, forcing the man to the ground, before he yanked Sam to her feet and pushed her into a run ahead of him. "Deeper into the trees."

The noise of the snowmobiles ebbed to an idling growl as they reached the barrier of the tree line. The woods would be swarming with the rest of those men any second now, and Sam was about to drop from a lack of oxygen and fatigue. The shouts were less distinct now, the enemy's movements harder to track.

But Whooping Trigger-Happy Man cleared his gun and stormed down the trail Jason had made no effort to hide. "You won't get the drop on me twice, soldier boy. Where's my money, honey? Come out, come out, wherever you are," he taunted, firing random bursts into the forest around them.

Pine needles and bark and tiny branches paid the price for every gunshot, sailing through the air and dropping like fallout from anti-aircraft fire. Bullets thunked into trees, exploded drifts of snow.

"I got 'em, boss! This way!"

"Watch your target! I want her alive. She's mine!"

"The hell with that! That bitch isn't gonna take a chunk out of me again."

Jason needed a rifle. Air support. A miracle.

This mountain is the only ally I need.

They weren't going to outrun well-armed mercenaries. Trees didn't stop bullets. But granite did.

Jason abruptly changed course and pulled Sam toward the lip of the rocky overhang.

"What are you—?"

"Hold on!" She tightened her grip and Jason squeezed his fingers around her wrist, dragging her to the very edge of the gorge. "Hug the rocks as soon as your feet hit."

"Hit what?" She screamed as he swung her over the cliff face and let go.

Jason spared a quick look at the men in black changing course in pursuit before he scrambled over the edge, catching a grip with his left hand and right toe, righting his equilibrium before dropping the last couple of feet to the narrow granite ledge.

Sam shivered against the rock face. "I can see all the way down to that creek from here. Oh, hell. That's a river, isn't it." Her voice was little more than a rasp of air. "My calculations say that gorge is about a thousand feet—"

"We gotta move." He pried her hand off an exposed tree root and pulled her along behind him as the rapid-fire staccato of automatic weapons tore through the air above the cliff edge they'd just vacated. It had been more than a year since he'd scaled the north face of the canyon, but he was praying that winter weather and rock slides wouldn't work against him. The opening where he'd rested before that last pull over the ledge should be about twenty feet ahead.

More bullets pinged off the granite at their feet. The men followed their path around the rim of the canyon, firing over their heads. The angle wasn't right to hit them yet, but they were getting close. If one of them figured out to run in the opposite direction, getting clear of the rocky overhang, he'd have a clean shot from the side.

Jason wasn't waiting for any of them to grow some brain cells. "Look at the rock face and step where I step. Don't look down."

"Don't look down," she repeated. "There is a way off this ledge, right?"

"Trust me."

"You can't just tell me yes or no?"

Six feet. Three. Two. Jason ducked into a recess beneath the rocky overhang as a final fusillade of whoops and gunshots filled the air with the stink of sulfur and anger. He hugged Sam to his chest, palming the back of her head and smoothing his hand down over her hip to pull the flare of her skirt between them, keeping any part of her body out of the line of sight. She huddled beneath the point of his chin, averting her face from the snow and tiny pebbles cascading past them into the canyon as their pursuers gathered above them. Her fingertips dug into skin and muscle, clutching him tightly as he moved farther into the darkness that neither the morning sun nor enemy eyes could reach.

"Get them!" That had to be the voice in charge. His order echoed off the canyon walls.

"I've got no shot from here."

"I don't want excuses. I want a dead body." Was it just his imagination, or did the boss's voice sound familiar? "Ten grand to the man who brings down that thief!"

"Ten? You promised us ten times that."

"For the Marine, you idiot. You won't get *any* money if we don't get her back."

"I'm not climbing down there. You think I have wings, Buck?"

"He killed Jimmy. All the more reason to end him."

Sam's fingers curled into the front of Jason's jacket. "Buck? That's the guy behind all this. The boss they kept talking about."

Jason nodded. The seed of understanding tried to take root. But solving mysteries wasn't high on his priority list right now. "Do you recognize that voice? How does he know I was a Marine?"

Sam was in survival mode, too, clinging to him as he moved them farther into the cave. "I'm just trying to not get shot right now. Is it important?"

The shooting stopped, and the voices grew indistinct as they put more distance between them and the makeshift army above them. But Buck's orders were clear. "Grab the rappelling gear. We'll trap them inside. Smoke 'em out. You—get me anything that will burn. You—if that guy pops his head out? Shoot it."

"What about the girl?"

"Wing her if you have to. But I'm the one who gets to cut out her heart and serve it to Daddy."

Sam's weight sagged against him at the venomous directive, as if her knees were suddenly too weak to stand. "That sounds a little hateful."

"I didn't sign on for cold-blooded murder, Buck," one of the men groused.

Buck didn't seem to hear the protest. "You get me Walter Eddington on the phone. I don't appreciate him playing games like this. He needs to know the price for getting his daughter back just went up."

"That means hiking back to the truck and driving down the mountain."

"Then get to it!" Buck shouted. "He needs to know I'm carving up another piece of his daughter now for thinking he could get away without paying me. And I want to tell him in explicit detail how much I'm going to enjoy doing it."

"I don't want to kill anybody. Jimmy's already dead. Plus, that guy in the chopper." There was a buzz of conversation overhead, the shuffling of men and equipment. But the man who wanted out was louder than the rest. "Cut me out of the money if you want to. She can't ID us, and you know I won't talk—my pledge is still good. But I'm headin' home."

Jason heard a brief, unexpected moment of silence. Then even he jumped at the crack of a bullet. A corresponding thump gave way to another shower of gravel at the mouth of the cave.

Ah, hell.

"Anybody else want to argue with me?" Buck challenged.

A man's limp body splatted onto the ledge at the lip of the cave. Samantha screamed at the bloody, blank-eyed face that stared at them for a few seconds before his momentum carried him over the edge into the abyss.

She turned her face into Jason's chest, muffling her next screaming sob. Yeah, these guys were a whole different kind of crazy than poor Marty had suspected when he'd signed them up for this rescue mission. *Buck* had no regard for human life, even a friend's. He was mission-oriented, with his own agenda. And Jason seriously doubted that this was about the money for him. At least, it wasn't *just* about the money. Kidnapping Sam was about pain and punishment. Although if Sam or her father or some other cause was the source of his rage, he couldn't tell. But he understood one thing—the only way Buck wanted this sortie to end was with Sam and Jason dead. And he had the numbers and firepower to do just that.

Judging by the way she clung to his jacket and sagged against him, Sam understood that, too. Tightening his hold around her waist to keep her on her feet, Jason pulled her deeper into the cave. "This way."

"I'm comin' for you, Samantha," Buck's fading voice taunted. Buck's men were scrambling to obey his commands now. "Get those torches lit. I want a rope here, now!"

Jason still had Sam tucked beneath his arm, their deep, ragged breaths falling into sync as a snowmobile fired up, kicking up another fall of snow and debris beyond the mouth of the cave. The voices faded. Jason paused to unzip a cargo pocket on his thigh.

"I can't see anything," Sam whispered. Thankfully, she hadn't collapsed into tears, and the screams had been more about shock than debilitating fear. "It doesn't sound like they're all going away. Are you sure you know what you're doing? We can't hide in here forever."

"They only think we're trapped." Jason pulled out his flashlight and clicked it on, shining the light into the space between them, quickly assessing the pallor of her skin and how well she was breathing, before covering one of her hands where it rested against his jacket. "I won't let anything happen to you," he promised. "I *can't* let anything happen."

A frown puckered the skin above the bridge of her glasses. "Can't?"

"I'm not losing anybody else on my watch. Come on." Lacing his fingers through hers, Jason turned the light farther into the cave and led her over a formation of broken rock that blocked them from view of the cave opening. They shimmied through a narrow crevasse before reaching an opening where the cave branched off in three different directions. One led back to the cliff face, and the other was a dead end. He paused a moment to orient himself to the correct option.

"My dad must be paying you an awful lot of

money to risk your life like this for me," Sam suggested, adjusting her glasses to peer into the darkness with him.

"I'm not doing it for the money." That way.

She planted her feet, tugging him to a halt. "Then why?"

Jason swung the beam of the flashlight back to her face. "Let's just say I'm repaying a debt I owe."

"To Dad? To Marty? Is this a Band of Brothers kind of thing?"

"Partly."

The frown reappeared. "I don't understand."

And this wasn't the time or place to explain. Buck wasn't all that different from the terrorists who'd taken hostages over in Kilkut. And though he blanked the worst of the memories from his mind, the essence of the danger they were facing remained. He had to think like a Marine. He wouldn't resort to Buck's extreme methods of persuasion, but he needed Sam to obey every order.

With a faint pink coloring her skin again, and the distant din of men and gear overhead reminding him they had only a few minutes to rest, he slipped his fingers beneath the necklace hanging at the front of her coat, catching the carved silver locket in his palm. "This means you're supposed to trust me. Remember?"

She wrapped her fingers around his hand, capturing him and the locket he held inside. Even in this dim light, he could see her eyes were far from certain. "I take it there's another way out of this cave?

And you're not just leading me down into the dark, scary place so we can die later?"

Jason nodded. "I need you to go on being tougher than you ever thought you could be, and do as I say for a little while longer."

She glanced toward the narrow slant of blackness leading into the deepest part of the cave. "No hibernating bears or other surprises?"

"Can't promise that. That passageway is too narrow for bears. It's coming out the other side where we'll have to be careful."

"Do you have bear spray?"

"I do. And you have me."

She nodded, looking not at all convinced that either his word or his plan were good. He leaned in, obeying instinct, even though an inner voice of experience warned him this was a dangerous miscalculation, and pressed his lips against the cool skin of her forehead. He lingered there until he felt the pucker of her frown relax. And before that voice of reason could scream any louder, he dipped his head and brushed his lips across the soft curve of her mouth. He breathed in her startled gasp and tugged at the fluttering pulse of her full lower lip.

Her lips closed around his bottom lip, capturing it for a moment in her gentle grasp, waking something dormant and faintly animalistic in response to her tender acceptance. He traced the lean line of her top lip with his tongue. And while he took little nibbles along the same path, she stroked that decadent bottom lip against the scruff of his beard and captured his lip again and again. A sound, like the whimper of a baby animal, hummed in her throat, and she smiled against his skin, as if she was enjoying learning the texture of his face as much as he was enjoying this brief respite from danger, guilt and grief.

But the distant rumble of a snowmobile speeding away across the mountain above them was far louder than any voice inside his head, and he pulled away. "We'd better go."

"You kissed me." Her voice was a breathy sigh that revealed curiosity rather than surprise.

"Yeah? You kissed me back."

"Wasn't I supposed to? I mean, I wanted to." Sam shook her head. "I don't understand you," she admitted, testing the feel of him on her lips with the tip of her tongue. It was an unconsciously sexy gesture that warmed his blood all the way down to his toes with the urge to stamp a more thorough claim on her mouth and discover what she'd be like if he tapped into the passion he suspected was locked up inside her.

An imaginary hand slapped him up the side of his head as he remembered something important. "Sorry. I know you have a fiancé or boyfriend or something."

"Not anymore."

Jason frowned. "What was his name? Grazer? He was at the meeting where your father hired me."

"Scumbag," she muttered. "I suppose he was acting all brokenhearted at my disappearance."

His gaze narrowed at the roll of her eyes. "I'd say

pissed off was more his reaction. He was adamant that your father pay the ransom to get you back."

"My father should pay *him* the money to get him out of my life. Lousy excuse for a man. He undermined my confidence... When I broke up with him, do you know what he said to me?" Her gaze dropped to the middle of his chest. "I don't want to talk about it."

There was something out there she wouldn't discuss? While her condemnation of her ex triggered both relief and concern—neither of which he should be feeling—and reinforced his low opinion of the hotheaded Grazer, Jason was getting used to her rambling tangents filling up the dead space when he had nothing to say. But who was he to urge anyone to talk about things they didn't want to. "Fair enough."

"I'm grateful that you came for me. If I question too many of your dictates, or it seems like I'm arguing, it's just because it's my nature." She twirled her finger beside her head in a universal sign for crazy. "Logical, science-y, engineer brain. I like facts. Not real good at trusting my instincts and reading people, though. But I trust you."

That was what he wanted, right? Her complete faith in him so she wouldn't question any command required to keep her safe? Elaine had trusted him to come to her rescue and save her. Every man in his unit had trusted him to have their back and lead them safely home.

Jason tilted his head to the cave's damp, black ceiling, taking a moment to get his head back in the survival game before he blew this mission, too. "All right, then. Let's move out before Buck and his men rappel down the cliff and figure out which of these passages cuts through to the other side of the gorge."

"*You* know, though, right?" She waved off that moment of doubt. "I said I trust you, and I do. How many rules are we up to now? Six or seven? Keep moving? Step where you step? I've got them memorized now."

"Don't let go of my hand." He couldn't risk her getting turned around and wandering away down the wrong passage.

"No problem with that," she assured him, latching on with both hands. "Lead on."

As Sam willingly followed him into the darkness, he wondered if her ready trust in him would be an even more dangerous mistake than that kiss.

Chapter Seven

Samantha's feet felt like stones at the end of her frozen, boneless legs, dragging through the snow and tufts of brown grass peeking through along the ridge above the South Fork of Cascade Canyon.

Her nose was an ice cube in the middle of her face. Her body was bruised; her skin was chapped. Her shoulder where she'd been cut open to remove her tracking chip ached, and she was certain she was never getting the body-hugging undergarment she wore tugged back into the right places after that last stop to relieve herself, and so things were chafing in uncomfortable places. Her stomach growled with hungry protest. And Jason wasn't talking.

Not that he'd proved himself to be a brilliant conversationalist in the twelve hours she'd known him thus far. But she preferred him barking orders or laying down rules or tossing her over the edge of a cliff without a proper warning to this stoic silence.

No. She preferred him kissing her. Swallowing up both her hands in one of his. Hugging her so tightly to his chest that she knew every bump and hollow of equipment, weapons, clothing and muscle the man carried with such sexy, unapologetically male ease.

She wondered if Jason Hunt even owned a tie. She couldn't imagine the rugged outdoorsman and former Marine wearing anything close to the tuxedos and tailored suits Kyle favored. Not that he needed any fancy adornment to draw her eyes to those broad shoulders and the tight lift of his butt in those cargo hiking pants she'd followed the last countless miles since leaving the claustrophobic chill of the cave.

It had taken just one of those twelve hours for her to admit she was attracted to him. Even a nerd like her could appreciate tall, dark and not-quite-handsome. Another hour and she'd learned to appreciate his unique skill set as a survivalist, sharpshooter and bodyguard. After only a few hours of knowing him, she felt compassion for the shadows that went beyond the loss of a former comrade that haunted his granite-colored eyes, along with a curious need to know what had put those shadows there and how she could make them go away. His praise was sparing, but genuine, instilling her with more confidence than any of the pretty poetry Kyle had used on her. Patience might not be his strong suit, but he made an effort to explain most of his actions and teach her a few survival skills of her own, rather than telling her to *grow up and get a clue about how the real world worked* or to *fix* herself. At least he had up until he teased her skin with his ticklish beard stubble and claimed her lips in a kiss.

She still didn't know why Jason had kissed her.

Maybe he had a thing for four-eyed geeks with wild hair and horrid luck with men. Maybe kissing a socially awkward heiress or kidnap victim completed some notch on his bedpost. Or maybe he'd simply wanted to distract her from her panic for a moment so that she'd calm down and listen to what he was saying to her.

It wasn't lost on her that she was completely dependent on this man for her life. Or that his mood could swing from hero to heartthrob to hermit in the span of these twelve long hours.

Rule one. *Do what I say.* How was she supposed to ensure her survival on this fast trek to only-Jason-knew-where if he didn't give her any directions?

Other than the occasional warning about some bear scat or loose rock hidden beneath the snow, Jason's last words had been about the need to put as much distance as possible between them and the mysterious Buck and his surviving band of mercenaries. Yes, the route through the black, freezing, thankfully bear-free cave would make them difficult to find now, especially since they seemed to be avoiding anything that resembled a road or path. But discovery wasn't impossible. And until she was home in a hot shower and a warm bed, and she was certain her father wasn't blaming himself for her kidnapping or stressing to the point of a heart attack, she intended to do her best to follow Jason's rules.

She had rules five and six down pat. *Step where I step. Keep putting one foot in front of the other.*

But she was getting so tired. Tired of walking

and climbing and overthinking everything that had happened to her in the past twenty-four hours. She wanted to know who'd kidnapped her, and if there was any significance to being taken on the night she was supposed to get engaged in front of a crowd of dignitaries and reporters. She imagined she was front-page news. Except for the drugs and bullets and two dead men on the mountain, this might have been a whale of a publicity stunt. Mostly, she wanted to know whether being taken on the anniversary of her mother's abduction and murder was a stab at her father or just a cruel coincidence. She was tired of worrying about what the next twenty-four hours held in store for her. For her father. For Jason.

Despite the spectacular scenery of the Tetons on the cusp of spring, her vision had narrowed to the wall of Jason's back and the twenty yards or so of tracks and terrain between them. Although she was tempted to ask how much farther she had to walk, she tucked away the whiny voice and summoned the most sensible tone her weariness and sore throat could manage.

"Do you think it's safe to take a break now?" she asked, cursing his machine-like endurance, even as she wondered about the secrets and emotional pain he seemed to crush beneath every step. "I haven't heard a snowmobile or voices or anything but us for ages now. The sun was overhead the last time we stopped, and now it's in front of us. That means a couple of hours have passed, doesn't it?"

YOU pick your books
WE pay for everything.
You get TWO new books and TWO Mystery Gifts…
absolutely FREE!
Total retail value: Over $20!

Dear Reader,

Your opinions are important to us. So if you'll participate in our fast and free "One Minute" Survey, **YOU** can pick two wonderful books that **WE** pay for!

As a leading publisher of women's fiction, we'd love to hear from you. That's why we promise to reward you for completing our survey.

IMPORTANT: Please complete the survey and return it. We'll send your Free Books and Free Mystery Gifts right away. **And we pay for shipping and handling too!**

Thank you again for participating in our "One Minute" Survey. It really takes just a minute (or less) to complete the survey… and your free books and gifts will be well worth it!

↖ We pay for
EVERYTH...

Sincerely,

Pam Powers

Pam Powers
for Reader Service

www.ReaderService.com

One Minute Survey

GET YOUR FREE BOOKS AND FREE GIFTS!

✓ Complete this Survey   ✓ Return this survey

1 Do you try to find time to read every day?
☐ YES   ☐ NO

2 Do you prefer books which reflect Christian values?
☐ YES   ☐ NO

3 Do you enjoy having books delivered to your home?
☐ YES   ☐ NO

4 Do you find a Larger Print size easier on your eyes?
☐ YES   ☐ NO

YES! I have completed the above "One Minute" Survey. Please send me my Two Free Books and Two Free Mystery Gifts (worth over $20 retail). I understand that I am under no obligation to buy anything, as explained on the back of this card.

❑ I prefer the regular-print edition
182/382 HDL GM3V

❑ I prefer the larger-print edition
199/399 HDL GM3V

FIRST NAME	LAST NAME

ADDRESS

APT.#	CITY

STATE/PROV.	ZIP/POSTAL CODE

Accepting your 2 free Harlequin Intrigue® books and 2 free gifts (gifts valued at approximately $10.00 retail) places you under no obligation to buy anything. You may keep the books and gifts and return the shipping statement marked "cancel." If you do not cancel, about a month later we'll send you 6 additional books and bill you just $4.99 each for the regular-print edition or $5.74 each for the larger-print edition in the U.S. or $5.74 each for the regular-print edition or $6.49 each for the larger-print edition in Canada. That is a savings of at least 12% off the cover price. It's quite a bargain! Shipping and handling is just 50¢ per book in the U.S. and 75¢ per book in Canada*. You may cancel at any time, but if you choose to continue, every month we'll send you 6 more books, which you may either purchase at the discount price plus shipping and handling or return to us and cancel your subscription. *Terms and prices subject to change without notice. Prices do not include applicable taxes. Sales tax applicable in N.Y. Canadian residents will be charged applicable taxes. Offer not valid in Quebec. Books received may not be as shown. All orders subject to approval. Credit or debit balances in a customer's account(s) may be offset by any other outstanding balance owed by or to the customer. Please allow 4 to 6 weeks for delivery. Offer available while quantities last.

BUSINESS REPLY MAIL
FIRST-CLASS MAIL   PERMIT NO. 717   BUFFALO, NY

POSTAGE WILL BE PAID BY ADDRESSEE

READER SERVICE
PO BOX 1341
BUFFALO NY 14240-8571

NO POSTAGE
NECESSARY
IF MAILED
IN THE
UNITED STATES

Silence. Was this how he grieved? March on and ignore the rest of the world?

"Look, I don't know about you, but I'm starving. I haven't had anything to eat since that energy bar you gave me before dawn this morning. All I need is ten minutes to get off my feet and eat something. I can make do with five," she bargained, when he showed no sign of stopping.

Twenty yards stretched to twenty-five as she stumbled over some uneven ground and her pace slowed. She was getting a little light-headed. Probably not breathing right. Too much oxygen or not enough. Her lungs and brain struggled to find the right rhythm. "I don't know if you noticed this yet, but your legs are longer than mine. It wouldn't hurt you to slow down every now and then, would it? Jason? Can you hear me?" Either her voice was too raw to carry the distance between them or he was so focused on finding the safest route between men who wanted to kill them and civilization that he couldn't hear her.

Although they were gradually working their way down the mountain, the course he'd charted for them was more like a roller coaster—up one rise and down the next, circumventing one rock formation while climbing over another, avoiding one stream of icy water and hiking straight across the next one. As her stride shortened and every breath strained her lungs, she watched him climb a winding path through the trees up to the next ridge.

A flat rock sunning itself in a clearing a few feet

up the slope beckoned. Without the surrounding pines to shade it, even last night's snow had melted away to expose dry gray rock with hundreds of sparkly specks that beckoned like a neon sign. The ancient chunk of granite had been pushed ahead of a glacier eons ago and worn smooth by erosion. Samantha pulled off her borrowed glove and spread her palm against the surface. The sun made it warm to the touch, certainly warmer than the air around it. It wasn't her bed, or even one of the stiff new leather chairs back at the lodge. But it was warm and she wasn't, and the chance to sit for a moment was too inviting to pass up.

"I'm taking a break," she announced to Jason's back. He had a way to go to reach the top of that rise yet. She could make do with a two-minute respite.

Obeying the needs of her body, Samantha climbed onto the rock and stretched her legs out in front of her, relishing the warmth seeping into the back of her thighs and bottom. She heard the whoops and chirps of small songbirds, and the screech of a raptor—an eagle, maybe?—soaring overhead. She let her vision blur out of focus and listened more carefully. Underneath the sounds of animals and wind, she heard the splashing of water. No, it was more like splashing times a hundred. There was gushing water running someplace nearby. Someplace where the water was thawing better than she was. A waterfall?

This was a beautiful part of the country, she admitted. Rugged, hard, but worth the effort to see and hear and understand it. Not unlike her stony mountain guide. Even if he did refuse to talk to her. Or acknowledge her fatigue. Or slow down.

Her eyes drifted shut and her chin dipped forward until her head grew too heavy, and she jerked it back. She'd be asleep in those two minutes if she didn't keep her thoughts and at least some part of her body moving. Forcing her eyes open, she spared a few glorious moments to look straight out over the tops of the trees into the greening valley and frothy lines being drawn across a pond far below before her gaze traveled up the next slope beyond the dark tree line to the mountain's snowy peak. That pond was probably a lake. The creek feeding into it was most likely a river, maybe attached to the waterfall she heard. Those lines were probably boats motoring across the surface. If there were any people down there, they were too tiny to make out. Everything looked small from this altitude. She felt small, too, surrounded by towering trees and endless miles of mountains, snow and sky. "Get out of your head, Sam," she chided herself. A pity party had no place in her life if she wanted to survive this endless hike and the cruel, greedy men and dead bodies in their wake.

She was probably down to one minute now. Working as quickly as her gloved hands would allow, she pulled the pack she'd taken from the helicopter into her lap and unzipped an outside pocket. "Thank you, Marty."

Smiling at the pair of water bottles there, she opened one and toasted Jason's friend before taking a long drink. The next pocket revealed a stash of protein bars. She ripped into the first one and gnawed off a chunk of the bone-dry granola, oats and nut butter mix. She swallowed it down with some more water and felt it sink all the way down her gullet. It wasn't tasty or easy to eat, but there was something heartening about the feel of a food-like substance in her stomach again.

Rest, water and two bites of sawdust improved her spirits enough to risk conversing with Jason again. He was a tall gray figure in a black knit cap, pumping his long, strong legs from snow to grass to rocky precipice through the trees. "This tastes like cardboard, but I was getting to the point where I was worried the growling in my stomach would give our position away." No laugh. No response. She drank some more water, soothing her throat before reaching out to him again. "I am so eating a steak and mashed potatoes when I get home. What are you looking forward to when we get back to civilization? Are you a cake or pie man? Crème brûlée? A beer?" She lowered her voice to a grumble and forced down another bite. "Right. Super Scary Mountain Man doesn't need food or water or rest like us mortals do. Probably doesn't even know what civilization is."

Samantha cringed when she heard the words coming out of her mouth. "Sorry. I didn't mean it," she apologized, even though he hadn't heard her weary complaint. "Are you hungry? Do you want part of this? I can share…"

Jason was a good forty to fifty yards ahead of her now. Invisible threads of panic tightened Samantha's chest even as her breathing evened out and more oxygen reached her brain. She took stock of her surroundings the way a practical engineer would.

The depth of snowfall was thinner here. As their altitude dropped, the late afternoon sun was melting more snow, leaving gaps of bare ground and exposed rock instead of the oversize boot prints she'd been following for miles now. She glanced behind her, surveying the path they'd made through the trees. Even though she saw no armed men in black camo gear, she was too far away from Jason to feel safe. And if she lost his trail, she might accidentally wander off the edge of another cliff or come face-to-face with the bear who'd been marking this part of the mountain. Panic became thick cords that nearly choked her. In another ten yards, the people down below wouldn't be the only ones she couldn't see.

"Jason, wait up!" Samantha zipped the water bottle back into its pocket. Slinging the straps of the pack over her aching shoulders, she scrambled off the rock to catch up with him. "Are you upset about Lieutenant Flynn? Is that why you're not talking? I can't tell you how sorry I am he got killed trying to help me. You didn't even get any time to mourn. When we get home, I'll set up a memorial for him. Or help his family. Whatever you think is right." Her feet, back and leg muscles were really protesting now as she pushed herself to close the distance between them. Why had he set such a relentless pace? Had she said something to offend him? Did he know something about the men following them he wasn't sharing? Could it be…? Ah, hell. "Are you mad about that kiss? Did you break some gentleman's or mountain man's code? I didn't mind it, I swear. I liked it. A lot. It took my thoughts off everything else for a few seconds and I wasn't quite so scared. I know that doesn't mean we're dating or anything if you're worried about me crushing on you. No pressure, okay? I can pretty well guess that I'm not your type. It was just a peck on the lips."

A peck on the lips combined with that full-body hug and that rumbling deep voice that had tickled her skin and warmed her from the inside out. Kyle had had his tongue down her throat and her blouse unbuttoned, and she hadn't felt anything like the ignition point in the pit of her stomach that had jolted through her blood like a combustion engine turning over the way she had when Jason had teased her lips. It must be the thinner air at this altitude that made her think that kiss could have turned into something much more significant if he hadn't been so quick to pull away.

"If it wasn't a good kiss, it's my fault. I mean, I don't think my ex was that great of a teacher. I thought he was, but you know, there's a reason he's an ex, and I just never seemed to catch on the way he wanted, so he was kissing other women and boinking them and… Jason?" She froze for a split second when he crested the rise and disappeared down the other side. She was alone. He'd left her alone.

She wadded up the wrapper of the protein bar and stuffed it into her coat pocket so she could use her hands to balance and help pull herself up the slippery rocks. When she reached the top, she exhaled a noisy sigh of relief. Not a sheer drop-off this time, but a gentle, shadowed slope that angled down to a frozen creek bed. Indirect sunlight left the snow knee-deep as she half climbed, half slid down to the bottom of the ravine. The icy crystals got into the tops of her socks and beneath her dress, chilling her skin. But cold was good. Cold meant she was feeling and awake—awake enough to be concerned.

Jason stood on the opposite side, his pack and radio sunk into the snow at his feet. He stared into the blackness between the trees while she searched for a narrower point to cross than where he'd obviously leaped from one bank to the other. "Did you hear anything I just said?" she asked, carefully testing a protruding rock for ice before using it as a stepping-stone over to his side of the creek. "Please don't ignore me. I know I'm rambling, and I'm sure it's annoying. But all these thoughts are going through my head, anyway, and saying them out loud is what I do when I get worried or need to think things through…"

He wasn't fixated on the space between the trees; he was focused on the gnarled trunk of the lodgepole pine right in front of him. Her hand instinctively went to her torso for one nervous scratch.

"Is everything okay?" Samantha lowered her voice to a whisper as she crept up behind him. "Is your fist supposed to be up?" She stepped to one side after a moment with no answer, to see if there was some sort of message carved into the tree. Or blood or a chunk of fur or some other clue that told them they were in imminent danger. "I haven't heard anyone behind us since we climbed out of that cave, so I think we lost them. Did you find that bear?" She took another step, peeking around his shoulder to see his jaw clenched so tightly, it shook. Was he having a seizure of some kind? Was he angry? "I'm sorry I ignored rule number six and stopped back there. I didn't think I could take another step, and the front of my stomach was trying to eat the back half—"

All at once, he punched the tree.

"Jason!"

"There's a damn bullet hole in my pack and the radio doesn't work. I can't call for an extraction or radio our position, even though we're close to being within range. It'll be nightfall in another hour, and no way can we reach a search and rescue station, or get within cell phone range by then."

While he rubbed his bruised knuckles, Samantha picked up and eyed the broken device, wondering if the pocketknife she'd stolen from the helicopter had the right tool to open the casing and pry out the bullet wedged inside. Maybe the radio could be repaired. Finally, something she was good at, something that might be useful up here. "Let's not give up hope yet. Fixing things is a hobby of mine."

She ran her finger around the hole. That hole could have been in her. She glanced up at the broad target of Jason's back. Her snack sat like a rock in her stomach, and she suddenly felt light-headed again.

The bullet could have lodged in his spine or pierced his heart.

Although she'd known it, she hadn't really *felt* it until this moment—those men wanted to kill them.

"Hope? You're stuck with me, Princess." Ouch. Okay, she deserved that one for calling him a Scary Mountain Man back on the rock, even though she doubted he'd heard her. "And that sure as hell isn't the best news I can give you."

She knelt to flip over his backpack in the snow and poked her finger into the clean round hole the bullet had made. "Thank God the radio was there, or you'd have been shot." Losing Jason up here in the wilderness would surely sign her death warrant, as well. Losing him, period, messed with her equilibrium again. She shook off the dizzying emotions of fear and relief and shrugged the bag she carried off her shoulders. If it was simply the power cell that had been damaged, she could cannibalize parts from his flashlight and get the radio working again. "We'll figure out something else. Like you did with the cave and getting away from Buck. We'll walk all the way down the mountain if we have to. It'll be all right."

"All right? *Nothing* about this mission is all right." Foul words spewed through his gritted teeth. "It's *not* supposed to go down like this." With every negative word, he punched the tree. Samantha jerked at the violence of each blow, gasping at the pain he must be feeling. She shot to her feet. Did she grab his arm? Was she strong enough to hold on to all that muscle and stop him? "First I lose Elaine. And now Marty."

"Who's Elaine—?"

"Too many damn people have died on my watch. I *can't*…"

"Captain!" When he pulled back his fist again, she leaped into the space between him and the tree, bracing her hand at the middle of his chest. "Stop."

His fist froze in midair, his face contorting with grief and rage, his nostrils flaring as he sucked in deep breaths of brisk, cooling air. He dropped his hand to his side. Of course, he wouldn't hit her. But the tree and his hand deserved kinder treatment, too. His eyes, dark with the emotions that must have been building inside him as they walked, darted in every direction before his gaze settled on her. He pulled her hand away from the rough texture of his jacket and released her. "You can do better than me, Sam. You should have better than me to keep you alive."

Better than him? How could that be? What happened to that confidence he never once had to brag about the way Kyle had?

"I'm sorry about your friend." Tears made her eyes gritty, and she had to swipe them away to keep her glasses from fogging up. "I'm so sorry you hurt like this." She tenderly grasped his fist. He'd split two knuckles open and two more were swelling. "But please stop hurting yourself."

She reached into her coat pocket to pull out a tissue to dab at the oozing wounds. A single drop of blood trickled down the side of his hand and dripped into the snow. The moment it hit, he pulled away. But before he fully retreated, Samantha reached up to touch his face. She cupped the side of his neck and jaw, feeling the friction of his beard rasping against the palm of her glove as she tilted his face down to hers.

"Jason, I need you." His wild gaze snapped to hers. She felt the tight muscles vibrating beneath her touch as he held himself still. She gently brushed her fingertips across the sharp angle of his cheekbone, soothing the tension there. "I have no idea where I am. I don't know how to survive in the wilderness. I don't know how to beat the bad guys. I need you to save me."

He huffed a wry sound. "What if I can't?"

"I need you to try."

His splayed his big hand over hers, holding her against his skin. "My last mission…" He squeezed his eyes shut against a memory he couldn't shake. "Before I was discharged…" His eyes opened again, pleading with her. "I don't think I can handle losing anyone else. I can't fail again."

Samantha considered the best way to respond to the pain in that taut whisper. "Then don't."

"Sam—"

"Are we alive?" He nodded. "Are we lost?" He shook his head. "Then I'd say you're doing your job, Marine. And I have every reason to believe that you will continue doing that job."

Her reasoning seemed to take him aback for a moment. But then he nodded. He squeezed her fingers before pulling them from his face. "Nice speech. You're officer material. How tired are you?"

"What's the next stage beyond exhausted?"

The lines in his face softened with half a smile. "You've got a wicked sense of humor, woman. It takes a lot of spirit to make jokes when we're in such dire straits. Sorry I've been such lousy company." He stooped down to pick up the radio where she'd dropped it, then tucked it into his pack and pulled out a first aid kit. He opened a roll of gauze to tie around his bleeding knuckles. "I've...got some issues from my time in the service. Sometimes, I... I've got a lot on my mind."

Samantha pulled off her gloves and knelt beside him. "Losing your friend reminded you of that? The explosion? The guns? They triggered something inside your head, got you to thinking about memories that upset you?"

He nodded. "Post-traumatic stress syndrome. Marty's not the first man I've lost. He was air support for my unit in Afghanistan. He saved my life on my last mission. Even though I lost..." His eyes darkened and he turned away. "Marty flew in to evac my team when no one else would. Too bad I couldn't return the favor here."

"Those action movie bad guy wannabes are responsible for Marty's death. Not you."

"I do better when I'm not around people. Nobody gets hurt."

"You didn't hurt me just now when you easily could have." She smiled, taking over bandaging his hand. "I do better when I'm not around people, too. I don't mean to make light of what you've gone through. I'm just saying I understand the need to retreat sometimes."

"From your cheating ex?"

"Kyle? You were listening to all that stuff I was saying?" Feeling her cheeks flooding with heat, she kept her face down, concentrating on tying off the gauze dressing.

Her blush intensified when Jason smoothed aside a lock of hair that had fallen across her face and tucked it behind her ear. "Kind of hard to miss the conversation when we're the only two people here."

For a split second, she didn't know what to say. But then, as the thoughts tumbled in, her mouth started working again. "I knew something was off with that relationship. But on paper, he was perfect for me. I wanted to make it work." She shrugged. "I think my dad worries I'm going to be a lonely old maid. It made him happy to see me with a man in my life."

"Did Grazer make *you* happy?"

She thought about that. "Maybe at first. The attention was nice." But even then, she'd had trouble believing his interest in her was sincere. Only her stepmother's unfailing support of Kyle and his family pedigree had convinced Samantha otherwise. "I thought he found my quirks endearing. That we complemented each other. It never occurred to me that he was trying to change me into someone else. Maybe that's why Joyce, my stepmother, likes him so well. She'd been trying to mold me into a pretty princess for years. That's what she knows. That's what she thinks I should be. Looking back, I think the only thing Kyle loved about me was the vice-presidency that comes with marrying me."

Jason let out a low whistle. "That explains a lot."

"What does?"

"His behavior last night. He was desperate to get you back. Maybe he was just desperate to get his meal ticket back in hand. Unless…"

"What?"

"Grazer disappeared before the meeting with your dad and security chief was over. I thought maybe he knew something about your kidnapping"

Samantha frowned. "What would be his motive? Kyle comes from money. Why would he need it?"

"To get you out of the way so he could be with your sister?" When her hands stilled at the dark possibility, he took out a small pair of scissors to cut the end of the gauze.

Her dad had promised Kyle an important position in the company when he married *her*. But he could marry Taylor instead and get the same deal if she was out of the picture. How had this pep talk for Jason turned out to be about her? Shaking off the malaise that threatened to overwhelm her at the idea she'd been set up by someone so close to home, so close to her heart, she plucked the scissors from Jason's fingers and finished the bandaging job herself. "I can't picture Kyle going by the nickname of Buck. Besides, I would have recognized his voice if he was one of the men on the mountain."

"Things got pretty crazy there for a while. No telling what we heard. But you're probably right. Could be Grazer was just worried about your dad finding out about them fooling around. I wouldn't say concern for you was his priority."

"It wouldn't be. I was never going to make him happy. I just wish I'd wised up sooner." She exhaled her humiliation on a deep sigh before reaching over his bent knee to pick up his backpack and pull it into her lap to put away the first aid kit. "I have almost three college degrees, but I'm dumb about people. I have a hard time figuring them out. Who's being real? Who's sucking up to me? Who thinks I'm an asset, and who thinks I'm a burden?"

Jason watched her every movement, hanging on to every word intently enough to make her squirm. "You're not a burden to me."

"What would you be doing today if you weren't stranded on this mountain with me?"

"Working on my cabin. My dad and I started building it before my last deployment. I'm finishing it on my own now."

"What happened to your dad?"

"We had a falling-out."

She suspected there was more to that revelation than he let on. But he'd just revealed his struggle with post-traumatic stress—he probably wasn't ready to share whatever family drama had made him choose such a solitary life.

"My mom was murdered when I was a little girl. I still have nightmares about that sometimes. I was in the middle of one when you found me in the cabin. I don't know your experience, and you don't have to tell me unless you want to. All I'm saying is, I understand how traumatic events can get in our heads and mess us up." She clutched her fingers against her stomach for a moment, confessing every shortcoming. "I break out in hives when I get stressed. I ramble on to fill up the dead air because there's a very insecure part of me that thinks I'm not acting the way I'm supposed to be. And when I don't know what to do, I tinker or talk or make jokes or… get myself into trouble. The only thing I'm good at is being smart, so I get frustrated when I don't have the answers. People don't understand me. They feel sorry for me or I intimidate them, or the money does. I keep thinking my mom…she would have taught me how to be normal. My dad tries, and I know he loves me, but he doesn't know how to fix me. My stepmother's tired of trying." She zipped the pack shut and held it out to Jason, finally raising her gaze to his. "Don't blame yourself for anything you've done with me. I come this way—a little odd and eccentric, but tough enough. And I can learn anything if you give me a chance. We'll just keep putting one foot in front of the other and deal with the bad memories. Maybe we should make that another rule. No matter what happens—from the past or the present—we won't judge each other, or ourselves. We'll deal with it and support each other. We'll get through this. Together." She thumbed over her shoulder. "And we won't hurt any more trees."

His eyes held hers for an endless moment.

He thought she was an idiot.

He was probably still replaying everything she'd said inside his head, trying to make sense of it all. He was probably deciding right then and there whether she was worth the time and trouble and grief she'd caused him. Maybe he was even trying to think of a nice way to tell her to shut up.

But Jason did none of those things.

He dropped the first aid kit into his pack and reached for her. By the time she felt his hands on her shoulders, he'd covered her startled lips in a kiss. It was no tentative exploration this time, either. If he was trying to calm her down, the moist heat of his mouth moving against hers was having the opposite effect. His arms snaked around her waist, pulling her to him as he stood, lifting her right out of the snow.

Samantha fell against him when she lost her footing. Her fingers latched onto the collar of his jacket, hanging on as he speared his tongue between her lips. Her mouth opened and his tongue slipped in, swirling around the soft skin inside, testing the hard edge of her teeth before sliding against hers in a needy claim. He touched that unknown ignition point inside her again, melting away the shock of the unexpected kiss, triggering a tingle of heat in her blood and breasts and the notch of her thighs.

The tingling scattered her thoughts. Suddenly, Samantha wasn't thinking. She was feeling. She was learning. Jason was teaching, and she was an apt student, following instinct instead of logic. There

were no notes to take, no rules to remember. There
was just Jason and need and a kiss.

As the taste of him filled up her mouth, the scent
of him filled up her head and the heat of him filled
her entire body. She wasn't just hanging on. She was
grasping, pulling. Twining her tongue with his and
suckling on the firm lip that moved between hers.
She skimmed her sensitive palms along the rough
textures of his neck and jaw and tangled her fingers
into the thick strands of his hair. Jason moaned into
her mouth at the needy tug of her hands, and she
answered back as the deep-pitched sound vibrated
against her lips. His hands slipped lower, palming
her butt and anchoring her against the trunks of his
thighs, creating a friction that kindled even more
heat in sharp contrast to the cool air at her back, and
the crispness of their clothes rubbing the skin of her
legs between them.

This full-body contact was a new experience
for her. It was a graphic reminder of all the differences between male and female, and she relished the
discovery of all his hard places with her own soft
curves. Her nipples beaded to tight, almost painful,
nubs, and she felt weepy and heavy inside. The sandpapery stubble of his beard was a seductive abrasion
against the delicate skin of her lips, the stroke of his
tongue a soothing balm. His nose caught beneath the
rim of her glasses, nudging them up so he could press
a warm kiss to the apple of her cheek, the corner of
her eye. She kneaded her fingers against the back
of his neck before sliding them beneath the grip of

his cap to cradle the warm, masculine shape of his head and pull his lips back to hers.

She went after his mouth this time, replaying every nibble, tug and stroke that he'd used on her moments earlier. He answered every touch with one of his own. The give-and-take made time stand still. Samantha lost track of where she was. There was no past, no future, only now. Only Jason and this kiss.

And her rumbling stomach.

Her eyes blinked open at the intrusive noise and she pulled her hands back to his shoulders, mentally cursing the noisy growl of reality. She squiggled out of Jason's grasp, the cool air rushing between them as much of a shock as the initial kiss had been. But even as she sank ankle-deep in the snow, he steadied her with his hands at her waist.

"I'm sorry," she apologized, feeling a different, far less pleasurable heat coloring her cheeks. "That's embarrassing."

Seductive just wasn't a talent of hers. She glanced down at her smudged coat, torn dress, men's boots and knee-high socks. She knew her makeup was gone; her hair was a mess and she hadn't brushed her teeth since dinner last night. Plus, there was that whole never-ending question-asking thing that was probably bugging the hell out of him. Wow. She was all kinds of *not*-seductive.

He dipped his head to press a quick, dismissive kiss against her tender lips, pausing to study her expression for a moment before releasing her. "You okay?"

"Of course. Yes." She pressed a hand against another growl of her *not*-seductive tummy. "Hungry, I guess."

"You're right to let me know when I'm pushing you too hard." He unzipped one of the pockets in his jacket and pulled out a plastic bag filled with dried fruit. Opening the bag, he invited her to sample a pineapple, apricot or banana. "It's not the steak and potatoes you want, but the fructose will give you some energy."

Steak and potatoes? He *had* heard that whole whiny, stream-of-consciousness ramble earlier.

"Thank you." He tossed back a few bites, too, while she chewed and savored the sweet, tangy fruit. The apricot was more flavorful than the cardboard-flavored granola bar, but not as delicious as the taste of Jason. She stuffed the whole thing into her mouth, averting her gaze from the rugged lines of his face. When did she become such a devotee of kissing? And when had she ever thrown herself into an embrace without thinking about whether she was getting it right or not, or even if she was welcome to try?

Her brain seemed to be misfiring. Maybe it was the drug the kidnappers had shot her up with.

"You don't have to fill up the dead air for my sake. But if it feels better to talk, it doesn't bother me. At least I know what you're thinking. I don't have to be a telepath." Jason offered her another handful of dried fruit before tucking the bag back into his pocket. "I like the husky sound of your voice. I know it's not a hundred percent because you've damaged your throat. But it's kind of sexy."

"Sexy?" Had the man just applied that word to her? She choked the last bite of pineapple down her throat. "Me?"

"Nothing's wrong with your hearing, is there?"

"No, but—"

"Just watch if you get light-headed or dizzy. Talking expends more energy and lets more cold air into your lungs, dropping your body temperature faster." In the span of a few seconds, he'd kissed her senseless, tended to her needs, complimented her matter-of-factly and explained a valuable survival skill. What more could a woman want? Samantha followed his gaze as he glanced up at the sky. The sun was moving closer to the horizon. "And it will get cold again. The temperature is going to drop thirty degrees once night falls. We need to find shelter. Buck and his men shouldn't be able to track us after dark. I know a place where we can stay the night. It should be far enough off the grid to be safe." He dropped his gaze to hers, catching her staring at him. But her fascination with his rugged profile, ability to truly listen and his different sort of intelligence didn't seem to faze him. Or maybe he wasn't aware of just how badly she *was* crushing on her rescuer. "Let's amend that last rule. You believe in me, and I'll believe in you."

"I do believe you'll keep me safe."

He nodded. He made a scan of their surroundings, quietly slipping back into mountain man mode, into the serious, taciturn former Marine who had prom-

ised to get her home. He stooped down and handed
her the gloves to put on again. "You think you've got
another mile in you?"

Samantha exhaled a heavy sigh. "I guess I have
to." She pulled on the gloves while he adjusted his
pack on his back and checked the gun holstered to
his thigh. "Could you talk to me a little more while
we're walking?" He arched an eyebrow in apology.
"You won't talk…?" Wait, what was he apologizing for? He turned toward the steeper terrain that
followed the rise of the creek bed. "We're hiking?"
He pointed to the rock face, about fifty yards north,
where the water cascaded over a ledge, its plume frozen in midair. "We're climbing? That?"

Jason laughed, a deep, rich sound. She decided
then and there that he was just as good-looking from
the front as he was from the back. And she wondered
why eliciting a smile from Kyle had never given her
such pleasure.

"We'll deal with it. Together."

"That kiss was to bolster my courage to tackle
rock climbing?"

"No. That kiss was about thanking you. For getting me out of my head where I'm my own worst
enemy, and giving a damn about me even when I'm
being a total jerk."

"You weren't."

"I was." He helped her into her pack, hanging
on to her shoulders for a moment before spinning
her around to face him. "And for the record? You
don't need me to bolster your courage. You've been

through more in the past twenty-four hours than most people endure in a lifetime. But you don't quit. You make jokes when most women—hell, most men— would be crying. You're grounded, Sam Eddington. You were the anchor I needed today. You care—even when a washed-up nut job like me goes off the deep end. A lot of people run from the kind of scary I can be. You ran *to* me."

"It seemed like a matter of survival. For me." She brushed her fingers against the back of his uninjured hand in a tentative touch. "But, for the record—when you lost it, that really did scare me."

"Scares me when it happens, too. We'd better get moving." He tightened his grip around her hand, leading her to the craggy rocks he wanted her to scale. "And one more thing for the record? Sometimes a man just wants to kiss a woman. He wants to feel her in his arms. Feel her softness, her strength. There isn't always a reason. Your ex is an idiot if he never taught you that." He tugged her to a stop. "I don't know what lessons Grazer was teaching you. But there isn't a damn thing wrong with the way you kiss."

Chapter Eight

A fist of guilt punched Jason square in the gut.

"I thought you said you weren't hurt." The emergency lantern from his pack cast enough light through the murky shadows of the hunting shack off Pinewood Trail that Jason could see the bruises up and down Sam's arms, along with the shiner on her shinbone, scraped-up knees and the soiled bandage on her shoulder where her tracking chip had been removed.

"Jason!" It wasn't like there were any walls in this place. He'd already changed into a clean T-shirt and shorts before sliding back into his cargo pants and thin-knit sweater and tying on his boots. He hadn't expected to catch her half-naked. The arm over her sweet, full breasts and a hand in front of the boxer shorts she'd scrounged from Marty's go bag did little to hide her beautiful, battered body from his worried perusal. "A little privacy, please?"

He obediently turned away, although the image of every curve, every strand of toffee-blond hair hanging loose and finger-combed into unruly waves, and every injury he should have prevented was indelibly imprinted on his brain. It didn't help that he could hear her moving behind him, finishing a sponge bath with a moist towelette.

"I am so setting up a memorial fund of some kind to honor your friend Marty," she said, followed by a quick gasp. He peeked over his shoulder to see her hooking her bra back on and tugging it into place. "The water, snack bars and extra clothes he packed in his bag are lifesavers, as far as I'm concerned. And an unopened toothbrush? That's the best treasure I ever could have found. Jason!"

He held her gaze for a charged moment, feeling the temperature in the tiny cabin rise, even though he'd nixed the idea of building a fire in the structure's crumbling fireplace. He liked her better in that bra she'd rigged with straps from cutting up the girdle thingy that had cinched her body from shoulder to thigh, covering up all the best parts of her rounded, earth-mother figure. He'd like it even better if those boxer shorts she was wearing were his.

The rush of interest stirring in his groin finally made him politely turn away to face the door. Whoa. Where had that possessive thought come from? He hadn't been with a woman since Elaine. Hadn't really been interested in finding anyone—partly because he'd been raw with guilt and grief for a long time after Elaine's death, and partly because he didn't want to saddle anyone with all the mental garbage that came with getting involved with him.

But a day with Sam Eddington had him thinking about the connections that were missing from his life. She had him wanting to be physical with a woman again. She had him opening up and sharing things he'd talked about only with his therapist. She had him wishing he had the right to do more than protect her, wishing he could explore where this surprising attraction between them might lead. She had his priorities all twisted up in a way he hadn't felt in two long years.

But twisted-up priorities weren't exactly something he could indulge in right now. Not with Marty Flynn and his radio dead, and his cell phone useless until they dropped down another thousand feet or so. His extraction plan had been shot to hell. And eight to ten well-armed men eager to recapture Sam and kill them both lay in wait somewhere on this mountain, hunting them.

That sobering assessment of the situation was enough for Jason to set aside his interest in this oddly fascinating woman and remember those priorities. He faced her again. Job one was survival, not sating his awakening libido or respecting her Puritan need for privacy. She was using the Swiss Army knife she'd taken out of the chopper to cut a length of cord she'd slipped through the belt loops of the man-sized jeans to cinch them around her waist. She chided him with a silent glare before turning her back on him to roll up the pant legs to her ankles.

"Don't get many women up here in this neck of the woods, huh?" she tried to joke. "Is that why you keep staring at my girlie parts?"

"Stop." He wasn't in a joking mood. The gauze bandage that had been taped over her shoulder was caked with blood and had come loose. He closed the distance between them in three short strides. "I want to check your injuries before you get completely dressed. Especially that cut on your shoulder. Looks like it's been bleeding. You should have told me the pack was rubbing against it."

She batted his hand away and picked up the gray T-shirt that had also been rolled up in Marty's pack, clutching it in front of her like a shield. "So you could carry both packs? It's bad enough I got you into this mess. I want to do my part to help."

"You didn't get me into anything I didn't volunteer for."

"Yes, but you thought you'd be home in your cozy little bed tonight. You weren't expecting so many well-armed men to be waiting for us. And I know you didn't expect them to kill your friend." No. This supposedly easy op had gone south almost from the get-go. When he didn't respond, she reached out, probably to share more of the compassion she needed to keep for her own strength. Needing to take care of her more than he needed taking care of, Jason moved away to pull the first aid kit out of his own pack. Rebuffing her concern only made Sam transfer her worries in another direction. "Do you think Dad has called in reinforcements by now? Other members of your search and rescue team? Pellegrino and his men? The sheriff's department? FBI?"

Jason pulled out the supplies and set them on the

pine bench that passed for a seating area in the old shack. "I hope not. They have no idea of the kind of firepower they'd be running into up here, and we have no way to warn them. At this point, it's easier, and probably safer, for us to hide and wait out Buck than it is to try to coordinate a new rescue plan. We'll send the authorities in to round them up once I know you're safe."

"Dad must be worried sick that he hasn't heard from us. He has a heart condition, you know. I hope Joyce is making him take all his meds because the stress could kill him." Her eyes were focused on some far-off place as she pulled on the T-shirt. "The similarities between last night and my mom's kidnapping are creepy. They feel almost intentional. She and Dad were at a party like I was. She left early by herself because she wasn't feeling well. Never made it home. It was a business reception celebrating his first new builds in Wyoming—just outside Yellowstone and Teton."

"The land Cordes accused him of stealing?" Sam looked surprised that he knew that, so he explained. "Richard Jr. was at the bar where I met your father last night. The two of them were arguing when I walked in."

Sam's cheeks went a scary shade of pale. "Did he hurt Dad? Threaten him? Do you think he's behind my kidnapping? In retaliation for his father's execution?"

"Pellegrino and his boy Metz kept Cordes away from your father." Jason made no mention of the role he'd played in breaking up the fight. It hadn't been any big deal to step in where he'd been needed. But it wasn't modesty that left him analyzing the antagonistic behavior he'd seen at Kitty's. "I've never known Junior to go by *Buck*. And he didn't seem interested in your father's money. Plus, he's got an airtight alibi for the time you were abducted. But I don't like coincidences like that."

"Maybe he hired those men to kidnap me. Maybe Buck's a friend of his."

"Or a cousin. Lord knows there are enough of Cordes's old militia group, their kids and grandkids, still scattered around the area."

"It sounded like this was personal for Buck. You think this is about revenge instead of money?" She sank onto the far end of the bench. "Dad already blames himself for Mom's death. I know he's blaming himself for me. Hasn't he been hurt enough?" Her gaze kicked up to Jason's. "I have to get a hold of him and let him know I'm okay. I have to get home."

Did she ever think of herself first?

"One step at a time, Sam," he cautioned, straddling the opposite end of the bench. "I want to keep you in one piece first."

"Do you think the kidnappers contacted him at noon like they originally planned? Even though I wasn't there to make the video for them? I can imagine they'd say some vile things to upset him. Maybe even lie and say they'd already killed me because he wouldn't pay the ransom. They could have videotaped me when I was passed out from the drugs—I probably looked dead."

Jason remembered his own advice to himself. "Priorities, Sam. We'll figure out the who and how later. And I promise we'll contact your dad as soon as we're in cell range. But right now, we need rest. And I want to err on the side of caution and check your injuries. It's not like there's an emergency room I can take you to up here if an infection sets in. We're still a full day's hike down to civilization—and that's only if we don't run into Buck and his friends again."

Nodding, she let him steer the conversation away from her concern for her father. "All right. I'll let you tend my wounds if you let me change the dressing on your hand and check that spot where the flying helicopter part burned through your pant leg."

"The metal was hot enough, I'm sure it cauterized the wound."

"Fine." She got up to retrieve the silver locket from the pile of her discarded clothing and looped the chain over her head. Then she reached for the moth-eaten sweater they'd discovered, along with a few other abandoned, second-rate supplies, when they'd searched the shelves in the cabin. "I don't take care of you, you don't take care of me."

"Sam." He caught her wrist, tugging her back to the bench. "We're doing this. You know I can out-muscle you if you don't do what I say."

"Yes. But I don't think you will. Despite every effort to be a big, badass Marine on a mission, I think you're a nice guy. The only time you've used your size and strength against me was when you were trying to save me, and you didn't have time to explain what was going on. Clearly, the fact that we're having this conversation right now means you don't have to rush me. Even when you lost it back at that tree, you didn't hurt me. And that means you won't bully me into something I don't agree with."

Sucker. Couldn't argue with logic like that. He released her and gestured to the bench, inviting her to join him again. "Well, then, I guess we're going to be playing doctor with each other."

Her eyes opened wide and she blushed, all the way down to her cleavage. Yep, watching that woman react to a suggestive remark or a simple touch wasn't going to get old anytime soon. He wasn't sure what she'd seen in Grazer, but he knew her ex was the one who'd lost something special when she'd rightfully dumped his selfish, cheating ass.

She sat with her back to him and Jason peeled off the gauze and tape and tossed them at his feet. He opened a bottle of water and poured it over the small, ragged gash to irrigate the wound. "This is going to hurt a little." She winced when he dabbed at the cut with an alcohol wipe but didn't complain. Without the means to put any stitches in the wound, he settled for gluing the jagged little hole shut, hoping it'd stay sealed once they got moving again. He covered it with a fresh bandage and cleaned and put ointment and bandages on the worst of her scrapes before he realized that she'd been quiet for an uncharacteristically long time. He helped her shrug back into the

T-shirt and holey but clean sweater before he tugged down his pant leg to let her put ointment on the burn that had indeed sealed the cut the shrapnel had made in his skin. "Just so you know, I haven't always lived off the grid. I've seen plenty of *girlie parts*."

"It sounds silly when you say it."

"It sounds silly when anyone says it." When she pulled his beat-up hand into her lap to unwind the field dressing, Jason captured the waterfall of blond curls that masked her downturned face and draped them behind her shoulder, so he could read the expression in her eyes. "If you're being funny, fine. But if you're denigrating that fabulously generous figure of yours, stop it."

"Fabulously generous? You mean I need to lose fifteen pounds."

"I mean, you've got the kind of body fantasies are made of."

She finally looked up to meet his assessing gaze. "Fantasies…? No, I don't."

"Is that something Grazer told you?" Yet another reason to smack that guy straight into Sunday for saying or doing anything to make her doubt herself or think she was anything less than a sexy, attractive woman. "He probably told you that old saw about women who wear glasses, too."

Ah, hell. He had. "He asked me to buy contacts. They're better for photo ops. And, you know, boys don't make passes at girls who wear—"

He pressed his fingers against her lips to stop her from finishing that untruth. "Men do."

Her eyes widened with the same anticipation that suddenly raced through his blood like a fast-running river breaking through an ice jam.

And then he replaced his fingers with his lips, claiming her soft, responsive mouth. Her welcome was instant and unhesitating. Her fingers cupped the side of his jaw, stroking against the beard stubble there, pressing into the skin and muscle underneath. He tunneled his fingers through the weight of her hair and clasped the nape of her neck, drawing her into the vee between his legs, knocking trash and the first aid box to the floor as he lifted her onto his lap. He'd never had an addiction before, but kissing Sam was quickly becoming something Jason couldn't say no to.

She tasted like minty toothpaste and heat and hope. Her responses to his touch were as natural and powerful as the mountain beneath their feet. She mimicked each thrust of his tongue, answered every press of his lips. Innocent as he suspected she was, Sam didn't just meekly give back the caresses he offered. She ventured out into new territory, too, exploring his growling response to her teeth nipping at the jut of his chin, testing just how many times she could pull on his bottom lip and tug on his hair before he crushed her squarely against his chest and deepened the kiss.

Her breasts pillowed against him, her nipples pebbling into decadent little morsels of hard candy he wanted to touch and taste. Her breath quickened with every heartbeat, and that telltale hum in her throat told him she was enjoying this full-body contact as much as he was. Her exploring hands skimmed along his neck and shoulders before tangling with his hair again. Her needy tugs pulsed through him, heating his blood and stirring things up behind his zipper.

His lips scudded along her jaw as he tugged at her sweater and T-shirt to get his hands on bare skin. He found the nip of her waist, the smooth skin of her back. And while she was cool to the touch, his skin heated like fire when she tugged at the hem of his sweater and slipped her hands beneath to latch onto his waist. He skimmed his palms up to the edge of her bra and slipped his thumbs beneath the heavy weight of her breasts. He lifted her to spread her legs over his lap, nestling her feminine heat against the part of him that wanted to be inside her. He closed his teeth over the lobe of her ear and she giggled, a sound that was part delight and part overwhelming sensation.

He felt more like a man than he had in years when she responded to him like this. He felt more human.

He smiled inside at the pleasure she took in the simplest things. Quiet conversations. The tactile differences between his body and hers. The discovery of a particularly sensitive spot at the base of her throat. There was no calculated seduction in the way she kissed, no subterfuge he could misinterpret that might come back to bite him in the butt. Sam wanted to kiss and be kissed. She wanted to touch and be touched. When she tipped her head back, offering the creamy arch of her neck to feast on, Jason did a little exploration of his own, chasing that needy hum of arousal.

Jason slipped his hands into the tight space between them, rubbing her nipples with the pads of his thumbs and cradling the sweet, sexy weight of her breasts in his palms. "Oh, Jase. This is so…so good."

She squirmed in his lap, her hums becoming breathless gasps of pleasure that fueled his own desire. He reclaimed her mouth as he rocked helplessly against her. There wasn't a part of her body he didn't want to taste—no part of his own where he didn't want to feel her touch.

But this was crazy. This was piss-poor timing. It was selfish to see this lightning bolt of electricity arcing between them through to its inevitable conclusion. Warning bells from his past sounded an alarm. He moved his hands away from bare skin but clutched the flare of her hips instead, pinning her thighs around him. He tore his lips from the delicious grasp of hers but ended up peppering her face with a dozen little pecks instead because he wasn't ready for this to end. Her heat called to his, and with a few flicks of his thumb at just the right pressure point, he could turn that humming passion into the release she craved. Would she come with a breathless moan? Would she cry out his name in that husky voice of hers?

Focus on the mission, Marine.

"Sam, we can't do this." It did him no good to indulge this need if there was a chance his feelings could get involved and distract him from the job at hand. It did her no good to promise something with his body that his broken heart and fractured brain might not be able to give. She found the button of his pants and unhooked it, dipping her fingers into the front of his shorts, her knuckles sliding against bare skin. Jason had to grab her wrists and pull her free before he couldn't think with his brain anymore and this turned into a mutual hand job. "Samantha," he growled with a mix of want and regret. "We need to stop."

"No."

"We have to." He lifted her from his lap, pushing her back across the bench. He made a token effort to pull her sweater and T-shirt back into place, but when she scooted back toward him, he held up his hands to ward off the temptation of her primed-and-willing passion. "I'm sorry." His nostrils flared with deep breaths, but he needed a slap of cold outside air to cool his jets and make this crazy craving for her go away. He gingerly swung his leg over the bench and stood, rebuttoning his pants. "I can't afford to forget what's at stake here. Your life."

Sam hugged her arms around herself, as if she was feeling the chill he so desperately needed. "Not the sweet nothings I was hoping for."

"I don't do sweet nothings." Jason raked his hands through his hair, pulling at the tangles she'd made there. The sharp pricks on his scalp were a welcome deterrent to the heat coursing through him. But the pain was an equally clear reminder of what a turn-on her grasping fingers had been. He forced himself to walk away to the storage shelves where he'd dropped his pack and jacket.

"I kind of figured that. I'm the one who's sorry. For pushing you into something you don't…that we're not ready…" Sam pulled her glasses off and rubbed at her eyes a moment before her face stretched with a wide yawn. "I don't have the energy to do this right, do I?"

Exactly. She was exhausted and probably not thinking straight about where this make-out session had been leading. He needed her strong to face the trek that lay ahead of them tomorrow, not drowsy and replete with the orgasm he'd wanted to give her. Plus, giving in to passion now would only make things more awkward between them when he needed her to listen to every word he said and take action when he gave the order. He turned his back to her, carefully adjusting his pants while he recovered, before picking up his jacket and shrugging into it.

"Did you want me to do something else?" she asked in a voice that sounded decidedly different from the *"Jase, this is so good"* that had nearly sent him over the edge a few moments earlier. "Kyle said I should be more—"

Uh-uh. Jason pulled Sam to her feet. He captured her face between his hands, maybe a little more roughly than necessary, and tilted her face up to his. He needed her to understand this. "You don't need to be *more* anything. I stopped because my first priority should be keeping you safe, not getting inside your pants. I stopped because I don't want you to feel I'm taking advantage of your situation. You don't have to give me your body to make sure I protect you. Even if you hate my guts, I'm still going to get you home." He inhaled a sobering breath before resting his forehead against hers. "I stopped because I'm not sure I'm the best man for you to get involved with. I'm not sure I'm ready to get involved, but I'm feeling like I want to, and that makes me wonder if my motives for lusting after you are as pure as they should be."

Her eyes darkened like a rich alpine meadow at twilight. "Lusting…?"

Damn straight. What did she think that was that had nudged against her thigh? Jason dipped his head and captured her mouth in a hard, quick kiss, reminding her that he didn't play games the way her ex apparently had. "That man's name is never to come up again when I'm in the middle of kissing you. When you're with me, I want all of you with me."

She might have swayed when he released her, but damn, it made him angry to think that she'd sat there evaluating every moment of that embrace, wondering if she wasn't measuring up to his expectations. Considering he hadn't expected anything to happen between them, he wasn't quite sure if he could explain the way being with her had awakened something inside him and turned him inside out.

Jason pulled his cap on over his head and strapped his gun and military-issue holster back into place around his thigh. She put her glasses back on and knelt to pick up all the medical supplies they'd scattered. Then she moved on to layering together a makeshift bed out of a moth-eaten blanket and a dusty sleeping bag with a broken zipper the former inhabitants of the cabin had left behind. He was geared up at the door when he realized she hadn't said a word for several minutes. Was she focused on her work? Asleep on her feet? Had he said something that hurt her? Ah, hell. Maybe his own ego had gotten the better of him here and he was assuming things about Sam that he really didn't know. Kissing him could just be some affirmation-of-life thing. Or maybe that logical, science-y engineer brain of hers saw kissing another man besides Grazer as an experiment, comparing what she knew with other possibilities. "Do you miss him? Were you thinking of him when I kissed you?"

Sam shot to her feet. "No!"

Thank God for that. "Then don't make me think of him, either. He hurt you. He used you. It makes me want to punch something. Preferably him." He curled his fingers into a fist, then flexed them straight, testing the bandage she'd wrapped around his knuckles. "You're better than he deserved, Sam. You're better than I deserve."

"Don't say that." She waved aside his protest and crossed the cabin to lay a hand on his arm. "Rule number ten. No more mentioning what's-his-face. Thank you for thinking of what's best for me. For both of us. It wasn't that hard to get carried away by the opportunity since I've been lusting after you, too."

He didn't need any games or tricks or coy seduction. Straightforward worked for him. "Yeah?"

"Yes." The rosy blush on her cheeks belied the directness of her upturned gaze. "In some ways, I can't imagine anyone more different from me. On paper, we just wouldn't work."

"True." She *was* a smart woman.

But before he could leave, she tightened her grip on his sleeve. "But in other ways... I can't imagine going through this with anyone but you. Maybe you're just tolerating me because you don't have any choice, but I feel like I can talk to you. I feel safe with you. And kissing you is—"

"A little rough around the edges?"

"I was going to say really hot. I can't always think straight when you're holding me—and I'm used to being able to think things through. I've never had chemistry like that with anyone. Certainly not with what's-his-face."

Jason laid his hand over hers and squeezed it. "It's the situation. Could just be gratitude or the thrill of something—someone—different, someone who's not part of the world you were running away from. Danger intensifies anything you're feeling."

"Or maybe it strips away all pretense and leaves you with honest emotions. I care about you, Jase. I think I care about you more than I probably should."

Leaving that bombshell hanging in the air between them, she went back to making the pallet. She rolled her sadly abused party dress into a bundle and tucked it against the wall. Then she rolled up her checkered coat and set the bundles side by side, making pillows for them both. Without a fire to warm them, he'd recommended they share a bed and their body heat tonight. She'd agreed, saying that sleeping together was a sensible solution. Despite the limited, no-frills resources available to them, the domestic picture she made left Jason wondering which of them was right. Were they attracted to each other *because* of the circumstances surrounding them? Or *despite* them? In the outside world, where she was a society princess and he was a recluse, where she worked with her brain and he worked with his hands, where she was close to her family and he was estranged from his, would they have anything in common? Would they even have noticed each other? Would he be feeling this inexplicable pull toward hope and salvation that Sam seemed to offer? Would he have spent enough time getting to know her that he'd look beyond the geeky exterior to discover her intriguing mix of brave compassion and almost shy vulnerability?

"Who's Elaine...?"

The question jerked Jason from his thoughts. Wow. That woman sure knew how to throw an emotional punch. Maybe he needed to rethink that straightforward quality he admired.

She hugged the Mylar blanket from his pack to her chest. "You mentioned her when you were giving the tree a beat-down. She was important to you, wasn't she? You said you'd lost her. She died?" He nodded. "Is that what happened? You were in a dangerous situation like this one, and your feelings for her intensified?"

That's how their affair had started, but after a while, Jason's feelings for Elaine had become all too real. Maybe Sam had a right to know why he'd wigged out on her at the tree. She was counting on him for her survival. She had a right to know why he'd ended that kiss, why keeping her safe was more important than any lust or emotions she made him feel. "I knew Elaine when I was in the Marines."

Sam spread the Mylar on top of the pallet before sitting in the middle of it. She hugged her knees to her chest, patiently waiting for him to answer her questions. "Tell me about her."

Jason scrubbed his palm across his jaw, fighting the urge to bolt out the door. "Is this part of that doctoring agreement?"

"Does it need to be?"

Closing his eyes, Jason inhaled a deep breath. Her expectant gaze was on him when he opened them again. He moved to the bench and took a seat facing her. Curiosity and concern created that pucker of a frown between her eyebrows. "Elaine Burkhart was a reporter imbedded with my unit when I was stationed in Afghanistan. I loved her. Huge no-no when it comes to military protocol, but I loved her anyway." He leaned forward to brace his elbows atop his knees, twisting his hands together as he unlocked the memories. "We had an affair. I vowed to keep her safe—we were in a dangerous part of the world, and she wanted to be on the front line. To get the real story. She'd been negotiating an interview with one of the imams in a village near where we were camped. Radwan. She was determined to present all sides of the story. Turned out Radwan was a double agent, connected to a group of insurgents who didn't want a military presence in their part of the world. Radwan and his men kidnapped Elaine, her camera-man and their two Marine escorts."

Jason remembered when their Afghani guide had run into his tent to report the abduction. He was al-ready suited up and ready to roll out on a half-formed extraction plan by the time the Major overseeing his unit had made the announcement and put the unit on standby until an official incursion plan came down from command. "My superiors wanted to negoti-ate their release. They didn't want to risk alienating their source to enemy movements." Jason shook his head at the precious time he'd lost. He should have risked a court-martial and disobeyed those orders not to go after the hostages. "You don't negotiate with terrorists. They value life differently than we do. It's about the mission for them. It's not about the people. They said they wanted weapons and intel in exchange for Elaine's life. The Corps wasn't about to pay it. By the time we got clearance to enter the village and raid Radwan's home…"

"Oh, my God." Sam was on her hands and knees, crawling toward him. "Jason…"

When her hands closed around his, he pulled her into his lap, needing something to hold on to. She wound her arms around his neck, weeping softly against his ear.

"They were already dead. It was a setup. We were all sitting ducks by the time we got into close-quarter fighting. There were villagers and insurgents, and we couldn't always tell them apart. I got Elaine's body out. We brought them all home, but..." His hands clenched in the folds of her scratchy wool sweater. "So many people died. Marty's was the only chopper that showed up to evac us out. I'm pretty sure he violated orders, too. I should have gone in as soon as I knew. Maybe it was already too late. I promised to protect her. And I let her die."

"No. I'm so sorry." Her hands rubbed at the tension in his neck and shoulders before she hugged him tight. "And now I'm putting you through this again. You don't love me, of course, but... A kidnapping? A rescue? Those men dressed and armed like soldiers? Marty?"

"I found you alive. And I will get you home that way."

She nodded as if she understood how much he needed to succeed with this rescue. After a moment, she sat back, pulling off her glasses and swiping away her tears. "You didn't kill Elaine. Those terrorists did. I don't suppose that's much comfort, though. You didn't just lose someone you felt responsible for—you lost someone you loved. And today, you lost the friend who helped you. I don't know what to say."

"It's war. It's a horrible hell of a thing a lot of men

and women have to deal with. It stays with you when you come home."

She looked him square in the eye, close enough that she didn't need her glasses to focus on him. "You're getting help with this, right?"

He caught a lingering tear with the pad of his thumb and summoned what he hoped was a reassuring smile. "I saw some Navy doctors. I've got a therapist in Jackson I go to every now and then. I've got the wide-open space and clean air of these mountains so the heat and small spaces and too many people I don't know can't get to me again." He studied her verdant eyes, absorbed the intimacy of her warmth and caring, surrounded by the silence of the cabin and night around them. This was pretty good therapy, too, and an unexpected calm centered him in the present again. "I knew this mission would push some buttons for me. I'd hoped I could handle it better. You need me to."

"I need you to be okay. I don't want to make your recovery any harder than it already is." She put her glasses back on and tucked her long hair behind her ears as if she was gearing up in a flak vest and helmet, prepping for battle. "I promise I won't die on your watch. I just have to follow the rules, right?"

Jason nodded. Hopefully, it would be that simple. Although, in reality, he couldn't even remember all the rules she was talking about beyond *Do what I say* and not mentioning what's-his-face by name.

"What about your dad?" she asked. "You said you

had a falling-out with him? I would think family could be a big help with what you're going through."

The woman could fill up the air with more words than he'd use in a week. Maybe even a month. But she *was* a good listener. She hadn't forgotten anything he'd said, not even in passing.

But he was still raw from sharing his memories of Elaine and Kilkut. Right now, he couldn't handle the shame he felt at being a third-generation Marine who'd failed his duty and come home without his head screwed on straight. "One touchy-feely conversation at a time. Okay? Besides, it's getting late. We both need sleep. I want to get moving at first light."

"Okay." She scooted off his lap and Jason stood, missing all the different kinds of closeness she'd shown him today. She shooed him toward the door. "I know you need some space right now. You go out in the cold and get your mountain man back on while you're checking the perimeter. But be careful out there. I've got an idea about how I can rig the door since there's no lock on it. At least we'll have a few seconds' warning if anyone tries to break in. I won't set it until you get back."

Jason planted his feet and pulled his gun from his holster. A jerry-rigged alarm wasn't protection enough against the danger that lurked outside, waiting until sunup to track them down again. He placed the Glock in her hand. "Your dad said you knew how to use a gun."

"He taught me. But I haven't held one for years."

"You afraid of it?"

"A little."

"Good. That means you'll respect it. It's a deadly weapon. I want you to keep it with you while I'm scoping out the area and laying a few traps of my own—extending your early warning system into the trees." He pointed out the important elements. "I refilled the magazine. I just put a bullet in the firing chamber. Don't touch the trigger unless you're ready to use it. Shoot anyone who comes through that door who isn't me. I'll be back in half an hour."

"But you'll be unarmed out there."

Jason pulled out his hunting knife. "No, I won't." Risking the temptation he hadn't quite been able to shake despite common sense and that nightmarish trip down memory lane, he dipped his head to kiss her again. The kiss was basic, brief, but he liked how she always latched on as if she was never quite ready to let him go. But she had to. No, *he* had to. Jason opened the door. "Stay inside. Stay away from the window. Stay safe."

Chapter Nine

The last time Jason had spent the night with a woman
sleeping in his arms had been that last night before
Elaine's kidnapping in Kilkut.

Despite resurrecting those memories so he could
explain to Sam the kind of messed-up he was, it had
also been the best night's sleep he'd had since Kilkut. He'd awakened a couple of times to make sure
the cabin was secure, but when he'd crawled back
onto the pallet beneath the Mylar blanket, Sam had
turned her cheek onto his shoulder and snuggled in
as if he was her own personal fireplace. He'd barely
noticed the hard floor at his back, or her soft snore
of exhaustion. Sure, he'd been aware of the heavy
weight of her breast pillowed against his side and the
light grip of her fingers resting against his chest. But
what stayed with him as the sun rose was that the
nightmares hadn't come—not one flicker of a firefight, not one raging shout, not one image burned
into his brain. Instead, he'd dreamed about big green
eyes and fishing with his dad and a fun night he'd

shared with Marty and some of his fly-boy buddies at a pub outside the base in Germany.

The bad memories had eased their grip on him for a few hours, allowing the good memories to surface and be discovered again. They eased their grip, it seemed, because determined, surprising, sexy Sam had never loosened her grip on him.

Peace was the best way he could describe what he'd felt last night. And he'd known far too little of that these past three years. He didn't know whether it was all the talking, being emotionally spent or having a trusting woman fastened to his side that had left him feeling this way. Sam's absolute faith in him coaxed at the trust he'd once had in himself to be the right man to get the job done. The woman was all kinds of unusual—maybe Jase-whispering was another one of her unique talents. Jason wasn't about to thumb his nose at the rare gift. He'd wound his arms around Sam's sleeping form and held on as if she was an anchor in the storm of his life.

And he'd slept. The way he suspected most men slept. Free from guilt and grief for a few hours. Content in the moment. Looking forward to the possibilities of the next new day.

He hadn't forgotten the danger on the mountain with them, the threats Buck had issued, the guns and casualties, and the fact he was the only thing standing between Sam and the men who bartered with her life without caring what a funny, smart, special woman she was. Until he could get within cell phone range to call for backup, or get her to a search and rescue station, it was up to Jason to protect her. As badly as he wanted to unmask Buck and find out who in her inner circle had set Sam up to be kidnapped, he knew his first priority was keeping her safe and getting her home to her father.

Although his motives for saving Samantha Eddington were a little muddled today, his mission was as clear as it had been the night before last. Checking the time on his watch, Jason hoped Sam had been right about the twenty minutes she needed to get ready to move out this morning.

He tightened the cap on the second bottle he'd filled after breaking through the top layer of ice to reach the clear, cold water of the creek and tucked it into his pack before tipping his face to the sky. Although the air still held the chill of the night here in the shadows among the trees, the rosy dawn had burned off the lingering clouds from the last few days of snowfall. Today would be bright and sunny and a few degrees warmer than yesterday's hike.

A warm, clear day meant three things. As long as they stayed dry, the risk of frostbite and exposure dropped exponentially. As they continued their winding descent and dropped in altitude, the snow would be melting or gone, meaning they could move faster. And without footprints and disturbed snow trailing in their wake, they'd be that much harder for Buck and his men to track.

Tucking the water into his pack, Jason looped the straps over his shoulders and studied the red fox that had come to the water to drink about twenty yards upstream from him. The little guy was probably on his way home from what he suspected was a good night's hunt, judging by the tiny bits of dark fur that dotted his muzzle. Jason held himself still, so as not to startle the animal before it drank its fill and returned to its burrow before the larger predators, like bears or cougars, came out for their morning meal. That little black nose and those wide, triangular ears were a far better tracking system than GPS or infrared technology. And when one of the furry ears flipped back, alerting to a noise in the trees behind him, Jason paid attention.

The fox scurried into the underbrush, and Jason ducked behind the cover of the nearest tree, quickly covering his tracks with the sweep of a broken pine branch. Tossing the branch aside, he tuned his ears to the sound of footsteps crunching over hard-packed earth and snow. That wasn't a larger predator creeping up on four legs. That was the sound of two feet. A man.

The fox wasn't the only hunter on the mountain.

Jason automatically reached for the gun on his thigh. But his hand slapped an empty holster. Damn. He'd left it with Sam. He crouched down, quickly assessing the man's location and in which direction he was headed. Buck's men had gotten here faster than he'd anticipated. Of course, *men* was a relative term. So far, he'd heard only the one set of footsteps.

This guy wasn't making much of an effort to mask his approach, so he hadn't spotted Jason. But Jason had no problem pinpointing the man emerging from the trees on the far side of the creek. Dressed in black camo like the kidnappers holding Sam at the cabin and the men pursuing them yesterday, he carried a rifle over his shoulder and wore a pistol at his hip. This guy's black stocking mask had been rolled up above his ears, but that didn't mean Jason recognized him, or could even give an accurate description at this distance.

But the guy had a walkie-talkie pressed to his ear, and his drawled response was loud enough for Jason to eavesdrop on the conversation, even with twenty yards and the rocky creek bed between them. First there was a crackle of static, followed by something about *blood in the snow* and *they must have stopped here*.

Jason eyed his bandaged knuckles, silently cursing his explosive reaction to Marty's murder. He hadn't policed the scene. Hell, he shouldn't have lost it like that in the first place. He'd let his needy reaction to Sam's insistent words and touch distract him from the basic mission—keep Buck and his men from finding her before he got her home to Daddy.

The clear morning air also carried the distinct growl of at least two snowmobiles in the distance. Search parties. That's what he'd do if he was hunting the enemy and had this much territory to search—split his men up and send them out in different directions to scout for their location. Only, he was the enemy this time. And he had no intention of letting any one of those scouts get a bead on Sam's location and radio back to Buck and his compatriots so the whole group could converge on them again.

One man he could take out. But facing off against seven or eight men by himself? That meant picking them off one by one.

Leaning back against the trunk of the tree, Jason unsnapped the sheath of his hunting knife. He hoped it wouldn't come to using lethal force, but if he couldn't get behind that guy and subdue him with a choke hold the way he had the men at the cabin, then he intended to do whatever was necessary to keep him from radioing in his position and calling for backup.

"Copy that," the man reported, moving upstream to the narrowest part of the creek to cross over to the bank on Jason's side. "I'm about a mile from the forestry service road. No visual yet. But the signal's getting stronger."

Signal? Jason paused in the shadows as the man moved up the bank into the trees. What signal? Had they found some other way to track them besides that computer chip they'd cut out of Sam? The man shifted course, moving along the edge of the tree line. Fortunately, the few boot prints Jason had left were farther in. But the man's course correction was far too accurate for his peace of mind. He was on an intercept course with the shack where Sam was right now. Brushing her teeth. Tying her beautiful hair into a ponytail and erasing all trace of their stay there last night. And Jason had no way to call her and warn her. Nobody was that lucky. Or that good at tracking up here. Except him.

He slipped farther into the trees, mirroring the man's path along the creek bed. He had to stop him before he found his trail and went to investigate.

"I'm going silent on my end," the man reported. "Switching channels to listen in. I'll call in when I get her twenty." The man twisted the knob to pick up a different frequency on his walkie-talkie. "This is ranger station twelve. Please repeat that request. Hello?"

Her twenty? There was no ranger station twelve. And no officer in the park wore anything that resembled a black camo assault uniform. Hell. This was no lucky guess. That guy had Sam and the shack on his radar, and he was heading straight for her location.

The time for stealth had passed. Jason needed to make his move. Now.

With all the lumbering grace of a bear waking from hibernation, the man hiked into the trees, his gear clacking together against his back, his boots breaking twigs and pinecones in the shallow snow beneath his feet, making it easy for Jason to slide around him without being detected. He followed him several yards until the man spotted the first print of Jason's path through the snow and knelt to check it out.

Taking his cue from the silent little fox, Jason crept up from behind and looped his forearm beneath the man's chin. In the same move, he yanked the rifle off his shoulder and slung it beyond his reach. Jason

cinched his arm tighter, lifting the startled man off
his feet, using the guy's full weight to hang himself.
He sputtered and cursed, clawing at the sleeve of
Jason's jacket. But the guy wouldn't pass out. He'd
misjudged the smaller man's bulk, forcing him to
use two hands to secure the choke hold.

But what the man lacked in brute strength, he
made up for in agility. When he gave up the fight to
free himself, he went limp, slipping through Jason's
grasp to make a grab for his pistol. Jason clamped his
hand over the guy's wrist, twisting until he cried for
mercy. But the guy wouldn't let go. In the two seconds Jason had shifted his focus to the gun, though,
the guy jerked his head back against Jason's jaw, the
back of his skull splitting his lip.

"Son of a…"

The gun fell to the ground. One of them kicked
the weapon into a bank of snow that clung to the
shady side of a rocky outcropping. The guy changed
tactics, jabbing the point of his elbow into Jason's
ribs, spinning around to land a swing-kick against
Jason's injured thigh. But facing him gave Jason's
fist an easy target, and he plowed his fist into the
middle of the guy's face. He felt the pop of his nose
breaking, stunning his opponent. Jason backed off,
swiping the back of his hand across his bloodied lip,
giving the dazed man some space as he stumbled to
his knees and landed face-first in the snow. Either
this guy was trained in hand-to-hand combat or Jason
was off his game.

But Camo Man was down, not out. Shaking off

the effects of his bloodied, broken nose, he rolled away from Jason, diving toward the rocks where the gun had landed. Jason didn't waste another second evaluating his opponent or his own rusty skills. When the man rose with the weapon in hand, Jason charged again, hitting him square in the chest and tackling him to the ground.

They traded punches and fought for control of the gun. They rolled over tree roots and pinecones. Snow abraded his skin and got inside his jacket. But the cold revived him. Sharpened his senses. He took a fist to the cheekbone and a knee to his aching thigh before he got both hands on the gun and smashed the guy's grip against the frozen ground. Once. Twice. On the third smack, his grip popped open and the weapon skidded into a snowbank.

Now Jason had the advantage. He braced his forearm against the man's throat, using his full weight to choke him into unconsciousness. The guy's stocking cap and walkie-talkie were long gone. His skin was flushed. His lips were pale. His bruised blue eyes laughed with arrogance as he stared up at Jason.

"It's you or me, bounty," he rasped, no doubt referring to the $10,000 promise Buck had made to get him out of the way. "It ain't gonna be me."

When he saw the man's fingers crawling across his belly toward Jason's knife, he pulled the weapon himself and put that to the man's throat. "Who are you guys? Who is Buck? Who wants Sam Eddington dead?"

Blue Eyes laughed, even as the edge of the blade

pricked his skin. "You better kill me, or I'll find your woman. Too much money at stake. Me or somebody else is gonna—"

"I'll kill any man who hurts her." It wasn't an idle threat.

The walkie-talkie, lying somewhere off to the side, crackled to life. A voice, husky and sweet and far too familiar, came across the line. "I'm calling the nearest ranger station or sheriff's department or search and rescue. Please. I can transmit, but my receiver is damaged. Is anyone getting this message? There are two of us stranded on this mountain. We've been hiking south from Mule Deer Pass. Men with guns are pursuing us. They blew up our rescue helicopter. We need help. Over?"

Blue Eyes laughed out loud. "Guess who she's been talking to."

Jason's blood ran as cold as the snow soaking through to his skin. Sam had fixed the damn radio. Just like she'd promised. No telling how far her signal had been broadcasting. Was this yahoo the only one who'd heard her or…?

Jason raised his head to the growl of snowmobiles. Not so distant now. "Ah, hell."

Blue Eyes was playing him for the lovesick fool he was. "Buck's gonna enjoy cuttin' her up. Maybe he'll make you watch before he puts a bullet in your head. Unless I tell him you're already dead."

He twisted under Jason's blade, slamming his knee into Jason's thigh, ignoring the shallow cut the movement sliced across his jaw. He kicked again, knocking Jason onto his backside before another vicious kick clipped his wrist and knocked the knife into the snow.

Blue Eyes lunged for his gun. He swung the barrel around, squeezing the trigger.

But Jason was faster. The shot burned through his arm as he scooped up the knife and thrust it into the man's belly. With a feral roar, he shoved to his feet, lifting him with the blade before dumping his opponent at his feet.

The gun dropped to the ground and Jason picked it up, tucking it into the back of his belt. Those blue eyes were wide, dazed, dying. "He won't…stop… He's sick with wantin'…to kill…"

"Who is?" he demanded.

Jason was bruised, breathless as Blue Eyes bled out. But he sucked in deep gulps of air, clearing his head of the violence, blood and death. He stooped down to clean his blade in the snow before briefly checking the burning gouge where the bullet had grazed the meat of his shoulder. Like the reopened gash in his leg, the thing throbbed like a son of a bitch. But he'd been hurt worse. He needed to move.

"I just heard a gun go off." Sam's voice held a tinge of panic as Jason dug through the snow to find the discarded walkie-talkie. "This is an SOS. My friend could be hurt. Help me, please! I need a ranger station or sheriff—"

Jason picked up the walkie-talkie and switched on the call button. "Damn it, Sam. Get off the radio."

Static was his only reply.

There wasn't any time to waste. Jason grabbed his pack, stretching his legs into a flat-out run as the growl of engines became a roar.

Chapter Ten

Samantha opened the screwdriver attachment on the Swiss Army knife and tightened the wire connecting the anode with the battery pack she'd cannibalized from the flashlight Jason had left with her. This should be an easy-peasy fix for her, but her hand shook. The reverberation from that gunshot she'd heard had rattled the false sense of security she'd felt since waking up with Jason's arms wrapped around her.

This wasn't some rustic Garden of Eden she was sharing with the rugged veteran. Yes, she'd had a good night's sleep. She felt closer to Jason Hunt than she'd felt to any other human being for a long time, and she was probably already more in love with him than common sense said she should be. Funny how she trusted him more than she trusted her own feelings. But feelings weren't the priority here. She wasn't safe. Neither of them was. She scratched anxiously at the torso of her sweater. There was only one reason why anyone would be shooting up here. And she wasn't so hopeful to think that a hunter had suddenly shown up on this part of the mountain this morning.

"Damn it." The shattered transceiver was beyond repair. There was no way to change the frequency, no way to have a back-and-forth conversation. She had no idea if she was talking to anyone but herself, but she stuffed the knife into her pocket and tried again. "This is an emergency. My friend may have been shot. We need help."

Samantha didn't hear the charging footsteps until they hit the wood planks of the shack's front stoop. She rose from the bench and picked up Jason's gun, bracing her feet and aiming at the door when it swung open. In one breath, she'd been numb with fear. In the next, she was light-headed with relief as Captain Jason Hunt of the United States Marine Corps barged in.

"Sam?" Her early warning contraption tangled Jason in a bunch of cords and noisy cans. Swearing, he pulled them off his body, ripping the nail they'd been connected to out of the wall.

She quickly lowered her weapon and ran toward him to help. "I heard the gunshot. Are you hurt?" She saw the blood wetting the tear in his jacket, more oozing through the stain on his pant leg. "You are. What happened? How can I—?"

"Flesh wound. We'll fix it later. How long have you been broadcasting our position?"

"You heard me? Who shot you?" There was dried blood in the scruff of his beard and a scrape across his bruised cheek. She peeked around him to look out the door. "Is he following you?" Finally free of her web, Jason caught her by the shoulders and pushed her to the center of the room. "Please tell me the other guy looks worse than you. What are you—?"

He knocked the radio off the bench and stomped it beneath his boot. His gray eyes drilled her for a second before he plucked the gun from her hand and moved away to pick up her coat and backpack. "How long were you transmitting that SOS?"

"A few minutes, I guess." She raked her fingers through her hair until she met the knot of cord securing her ponytail. Clearly, she'd done the wrong thing here. "I thought I was helping." She caught the coat he'd tossed at her, eyeing the shattered bits of plastic and wire on the floor. "You could have just switched it off. I don't think I can repair that."

He shoved her pack into her chest. "You're brilliant. I get it." He ejected the bullet from the firing chamber of the gun he'd taken from her and stuffed it into her pack, zipping it shut. She saw now that he had a second handgun secured in the holster at his thigh. Even before he explained himself, she was getting a pretty good idea of what had happened to him out there. "I don't know if anybody down in Moose or at the ranger station heard it, but Buck and his men sure did. At least one of his reconnaissance men was tracking you on his radio."

Samantha batted his hands away and took over gathering the loose supplies into her pack while he moved to the door to scan outside. She recognized the droning echo of snowmobiles in the distance. The hornets were swarming again, closing in on their position. Her entire body itched with regret that she'd unintentionally put them in this position. "I didn't mean... I'm so sorry."

"Your timing sucks, that's all. I shouldn't have snapped. I..." He wanted to say something more, but the urgency of the situation changed his mind. "They're on their way here. We have to go. Now."

He didn't need apologies. He needed her to move. She pulled her coat on over the moth-eaten sweater and hooked her pack over her shoulders. "I'm ready."

He eyed the top of her head. "Hat? Gloves?"

She pulled the knit cap from her pocket and met him at the door. "I can put them on while we're running. Hiding? Leaping off another cliff?"

"How did I luck out to rescue an heiress who doesn't know how to quit?" Heaving a breath laced with exasperation, he slipped his hand beneath her ponytail, palming the nape of her neck. She'd barely braced her hands against his chest when he pulled her onto her toes and covered her mouth in a hard, quick kiss. He squinted his eyes and grunted against her lips as if the pressure there hurt him. But he kissed her again before releasing her and letting her heels slide back to the floor. Then he pried her fingers from the front of his jacket and turned his grip to pull her along behind him. "Stay close."

She didn't intend to do anything else. "You're the safest place I know."

He scanned the clearing outside before jogging into the trees, retracing their steps down toward the creek from the day before. "Come on. I want to get to the river." Once he was certain she could keep up, he released her, allowing her the use of both hands to balance herself as they half climbed, half slipped down the steep, uneven terrain. "There'll be less snow there, and the ground is still frozen enough we won't leave footprints."

"The river? As in the bottom of the gorge?" She'd have to sprout wings and fly if he wanted her to cover that distance in a hurry.

"Creek flows into it about a mile from here. Before it hits the waterfall." She'd heard the running water yesterday when she'd stopped to rest, although she hadn't been able to place its location. But she trusted that Jason knew exactly where they were going. "Then it drops down."

"About a thousand feet!"

"A series of waterfalls, not one big one. There's plenty of river in between. We'll be more exposed, but we can cover the distance faster. Flatter terrain. Fewer obstacles. They won't be able to cross it with their vehicles unless they backtrack several miles. Keep moving. These rocks are loose." He pointed out the hazard even as he ordered her to follow him across. They created a mini-rockslide and Samantha glanced up the slope behind them, wondering if the noise and movement was loud enough for the men to track. She grabbed onto an exposed root to slow her skid toward the next tree trunk. Then she hurried after him toward the rock face they'd scaled the evening before.

"Thank you for explaining the plan to me." The consideration was a far cry from the bossy, taciturn man who'd pushed her to her limits without so much as a *please* or *You hangin' in there?* the day before. He wasn't a hard man, cruel and uncaring and all about the job as she'd initially thought. He was a wounded man, guarded with his thoughts and words and feelings because he'd been hurt so badly and had lost so much.

Yet he'd held her and kissed her and shared a part of himself last night. He listened when she talked, conceded when he could, and now explained when he couldn't. Samantha's heart pounded a little harder in her chest, and it wasn't just from the exertion of their quick descent. This was more than a crush she was feeling for Jason.

If she was completely honest, this was more than she'd ever felt for Kyle. Her feelings for her ex had been about excitement and discovery and the satisfaction of pleasing her father and alleviating his concern. She'd felt useful. She'd thought Kyle needed her. But that had all proved superficial, a ploy to gain her trust and make her feel something for him. On the surface, Jason didn't need anybody, certainly not a self-conscious citified brainiac who thought and talked too much. But now she had an idea of how isolated he was from the world—another survival tactic. She understood now that what he needed was compassion, acceptance, maybe even forgiveness for the tragedies in his past he blamed himself for. In all the months she'd known Kyle, he had never touched her heart the way these few hours with Jason had. Kyle needed her money and her connections to her father. Jason needed *her*. To listen. To hold. To trust. The idea that she could mean something to a man like Jason was as frightening as it was empowering. Although her experience with men was next to nil, what she felt for Jason Hunt seemed a little scary, yet it was more precious, more profound than anything she'd felt for the man she once thought she'd marry.

"Eyes on me, Sam," her beat-up mountain man reminded her, interrupting her thoughts. *Her* mountain man? Talk about errant thinking. He pointed to a knob of exposed granite. "That's your next hand-hold. Step where I step."

Focusing on the demands of the moment, she obeyed his every order, facing the rocks as he did when the trees thinned out. Although she imagined real rock climbing required a level of upper-body strength she lacked, he made it easy for her by pointing out toeholds and tiny gaps and protrusions where she could grip the rock.

Suddenly, the woods were eerily quiet. Samantha stopped, standing on her tiptoes on a small lump of granite, her gloved fingers flexing around the outcrop where she clung. She held her breath and tipped her face up toward the trees, unsure whether she should risk feeling relief. Had Buck's men gone the wrong direction? Had Jason's knowledge of the mountain saved them yet again? "Do you think we lost them?" she whispered on her next exhale.

"I think they found the shack. They'll be on our

trail soon enough. I didn't take the time to hide anything when we left." His hands closed around her
waist and he lifted her down to the flatter ground
beside him. The brief sensation of heat at his touch,
and the surprising flare of confidence she felt at discovering just how close she'd been to reaching the
bottom on her own, vanished as soon as he tugged
on her hand to get her moving again. "They won't
be able to drive down this steep slope. They'll have
to split up to cut us off one direction or the other or
pursue us on foot. And we're not slowing down."

Only, they were. At first, she thought he'd slowed
his pace to accommodate her shorter stride. But now
she saw he was limping. So much for cauterizing
that shrapnel wound. The bloodstain on his pant leg
was spreading, and the rip at his shoulder was oozing blood, too. Jason had clearly fought with one of
Buck's men. Had he been ambushed? Just how badly
had he been hurt? "Did you have to kill someone to
get away?"

"Him or me," he answered matter-of-factly. "I
chose me." She remembered yesterday's arduous
trek across the mountain. Yesterday, his strength had
seemed indomitable, his skills unparalleled. Today,
he seemed a little more human. A little more vulnerable. His breathing seemed more labored than it had
yesterday. Jason was hurting. What was this rescue
assignment costing him? And not just physically.

"He's the one who shot you?"

"It's just a graze."

He squeezed his hand around the wound on his left

shoulder, wiggling his left fingers as if they might be going numb. That wasn't a good sign, was it? His right palm came away bloody before he dipped it in the icy water to wash it off. That definitely wasn't a good sign. Samantha's heart lurched in her chest to think of all he had suffered on his mission to help get her home. But he didn't complain about the pain or what he'd been forced to do. He was a machine again, hurrying along the bank, testing which rocks weren't coated with a treacherous sheet of ice before climbing across and jogging up to the next line of trees through the snow.

Samantha followed along, grateful for the long, baggy jeans instead of the soiled dress she'd worn on yesterday's hike. The cool temps shouldn't sap her energy quite as quickly today. But it was still a challenge to keep up with Jason's relentless, if uneven, pace. "That arm's still bleeding," she admonished, unable to hide her concern. "You need stitches. Antibiotics, too, I'm guessing. At least let me pack it off for you. When was your last tetanus shot?"

The air around them was suddenly alive with the growl of gunning engines, moving closer. Snowmobiles. When they heard a series of rapid-fire gunshots and angry shouting in the distance, Jason cursed. Buck's men had found their trail again. Samantha turned toward the sound. With the noise echoing off the rocks and trees, it was hard to tell which direction they were coming from. She was only certain that there was more than one vehicle moving through the forest now. Had they split up like Jason had suspected? Could they be surrounding them? Getting close enough to shoot at them again?

She startled at the brush of Jason's fingers sliding against hers. "Less talking. More running."

Keeping hold of her hand, he hauled her up the creek bank and led her into the trees again. Despite his injuries, he lengthened his stride, forcing her to push herself into a faster speed.

"Is one ahead of us?"

"Above us. On the forest service road that runs parallel to the river. If he gets ahead of us, he can cut us off before we reach the walking bridge across the river. The others are searching the trees. They'll figure out where we are any second." He pointed to the right. "Remember downhill. That's where the river is. If anything happens to me—"

"Nothing's going to happen to you!"

"—go that way. Stay out of the snow and follow it. You'll be in cell range before you hit the next drop-off."

"I don't have a phone!" she gasped. A staccato of bullets thwapped through the tops of the trees over their heads. Instinctively, she ducked as bits of twigs and pine needles rained down on their heads. "Jason!"

"They're firing blind. Hoping for a lucky shot."

The shots were too damn close to be any kind of luck for them. "If they're shooting this way, they must know we're going to the river."

"There isn't any other way out of here unless you packed some rappelling gear I don't know about."

Another spray of bullets chopped up the snow a few yards behind them. "Jase?"

They were running now. Endlessly running. Samantha's vision narrowed to the broad strength of Jason's back. There was only Jason and running and deafening sound. Gunfire. Engines. Shouting. Their boots slapped against the frozen, hard-packed dirt as the layers of snow thinned, and every breath was a noisy gasp. Snow and danger was up the slope to their left. She caught glimpses of the river, of their escape route, off to their right through the trees now. But as the noises grew louder and the enemy closed in, it seemed farther and farther away.

But that distance was an illusion. As was the promise of safety. She could hear some of the words Buck and his men were shouting now. Or were those radio communications?

"River."

"Can you see them?"

"This way!"

"Nobody touches her but me. I'm the one who's going to make her daddy pay."

The creek and ribbon after ribbon of melting snow running off from the higher elevations poured into the river, and the river widened. They were close enough to see water splashing against the rocks and loose chunks of ice bobbing along the surface. But it was already too wide for them to simply walk across on stepping-stones as they had the creek. The current picked up speed as the water deepened, transforming the tinkling sweetness of a slow-moving stream into a thunderous crash of water against rock that vibrated through the mountain itself.

The loudest sound of all was her pulse pounding in her ears as her heart raced and her legs pumped to keep pace with Jason's. But he was faltering. She was lagging behind. Blindly guessing their location or not, the bullets and voices and snowmobiles were closing in on them. They'd never reach the river and the walkway bridge across it in time. They weren't far enough ahead of Buck and his men to get to the open ground where she and Jason could move faster. She'd never quite understood her father's love of hunting, and now that she'd spent the last forty-eight hours of her life as somebody's prey, she knew she'd never be a fan of the sport.

Yet as fear crept into her mind and fatigue claimed her body, the instinctive adrenaline of survival pushed it aside and cleared her thoughts. Her brain was her best weapon. *That's* what she needed to listen to.

They couldn't outrun bullets or snowmobiles.

She slowed to a jog. "Jase? I've got an idea."

A crazy one. Full of risk. Until they got off this mountain, though, every decision was a risk.

He snatched her hand again, urging her into a run. "We need to get out of this snow, so they have to move on foot."

"No. We need to go toward them."

"Honey, we—"

"Listen to me." She tightened her grip and jerked him to a stop. The fact that he winced at the sudden stop and rubbed at his injured thigh told her this was the right plan of action. She curled her fingers into the front of his jacket, asking him to hear her out. "You can't keep up this pace when you're hurt and losing blood like this. *I* can't keep up this pace."

His heavy breaths stirred a tendril of hair that had fallen out of her ponytail. "Then we're looking at a shoot-out, and the odds aren't in our favor."

"We have to outsmart them. Not out-shoot them. Can you take out one of the men on a snowmobile?" She picked up a dead branch, holding it up like a baseball bat.

"If we get close enough, yeah." Then his expression changed. Maybe not so crazy, after all. "Yes." Nodding, he plucked the branch from her fingers and took her hand again, pulling her up the incline toward the service road. "We need transportation. That's half a great idea."

"What's the other half?"

"Can you swim?"

"The second rule you said to me was that I shouldn't get wet."

The growl of the snowmobiles got louder as they neared the service road. "Right. You'll freeze. We'll both freeze. Can you swim?"

"Yes."

"Then I know how to buy us some time and get us off this mountain faster."

He released her when they reached the flat surface of the snow-covered gravel road that had been carved around the curves of the mountain to give emergency vehicles access to the wooded slopes, as well as create a natural fire break. Her attention was drawn to the ominous buzz of the approaching engine while Jason scanned the trees on either side of the road.

Deciding on his best vantage point for the attack, he led Samantha across the road, obscuring their tracks by dragging the branch through the snow behind them. "Get behind that tree." He pushed her back against the trunk, hugging his body around hers, shielding her from view from any angle. She clung to the front of his jacket, holding him close so that he'd be hidden from view, as well. "Be ready to go on my mark."

It was only a matter of seconds before the Arctic Cat and a now-familiar armed figure in black camo came around the bend in the road. Jason's gray eyes locked onto hers for a moment. He inhaled a couple of deep breaths. Steeling his nerves? Schooling his energy for the blitz attack? Reassuring her?

When she released her grip on him and nodded, he smiled. And then he was gone.

Even if she'd had a clear view of the road, the next several seconds would have passed by in a blur. The snowmobile was almost upon them when Jason charged, swinging the thick branch as if he was aiming for the bleacher seats. The wood caught the rider squarely in the chest, and between his speed and Jason's strength, the man went flying.

As the unmanned vehicle careened off the road and plowed into a snowdrift, Jason tossed the branch and raced toward the stunned man. The man in black staggered to his feet, clutching at his rib cage. He muttered something just as Jason tackled him and they rolled into the ditch beside the road.

Although Samantha's heart was telling her to go to Jason to make sure he was safe, her brain told her he was expecting her to stay away from whatever fight was taking place. Since securing the snowmobile had been her idea in the first place, she ran in the opposite direction. A quick examination of the vehicle revealed a dent in the front fender, but the gas tank hadn't been damaged, and the engine was still idling with power. She straightened the runners, climbed on board and shifted it into Reverse, backing out of the drift and centering it on the road for their escape.

"Ah, hell."

She shifted into Neutral and jumped off, hurrying to Jason's side. "Are you hurt?"

"I'm okay."

"Then what...?" She ran up behind him, resting her hand against his back and assessing the degree of pain on his face as he knelt over the unmoving man. When he didn't answer, she followed his gaze to the stocking mask he clenched in his fist and on down to the man's scraggly dark beard. There wasn't a single line marring his face. Samantha frowned. "He's younger than I am. This guy wants to kill me? Why? I don't even know him."

"I do."

When he didn't elaborate or change the somber disappointment in his expression, Samantha squeezed his shoulder. "Jase?"

The walkie-talkie hooked to the young man's pack blared to life. "Murphy, you got them? Damn it, cuz, answer me! Everybody, head east!"

She felt the energy galvanizing the muscles beneath her hand. Jason stood, towered over her, pushed her up to the road. "Get back on the snowmobile." As she straddled the seat, he climbed on behind her. "You know how to drive this thing?" Samantha nodded. This model was fancier than the one she'd ridden in college on a spring break ski trip with her father, Joyce and Taylor, but she understood how an engine worked. She kicked it into gear and turned in the direction of Jason's hand. "That way."

They zoomed down the road, zigzagging a few times to dodge the spots where the gravel was starting to peek through. Even with her glasses secured to her face by the knit cap she wore, she squinted as the wind whipped past them. Under different circumstances, she might have enjoyed the feel of Jason's hands at her waist, the warmth of his body at her back as they raced along in the cool, crisp air. But these circumstances were starting to feel far too familiar. Men shouting threats. That swarm of hornets, albeit smaller now, still pursuing them.

She turned her chin to her shoulder, shouting to be heard. "How many of them are there?"

"I counted eight to ten men, including Buck, up at Mule Deer Pass. They're down to five or six now."

"Won't they give up if you keep killing them?"

"Orin's not dead. He's unconscious."

"Orin? Who's Orin?"

She automatically ducked as a pop of gunfire shattered the air behind them. Jason hunched his shoulders over hers. "Drive!"

There was someone on the road behind them now, and he was picking up speed, firing random shots as he steered the snowmobile and tried to take aim. "I got 'em now, Buck!" he shouted. "That five million is ours!"

Samantha spotted a small supply shack marked with the forestry service logo ahead on the right. Jason tightened his grip at one side of her waist and pulled his gun from the holster on his thigh. She felt him twisting in the seat, reaching back to fire off a couple of dissuading shots of his own.

But trading bullets at this speed wasn't the only thing she was worried about. She could hear the thunder of running water skipping over rocks and breaking off chunks of melting ice as it tumbled over the edge of a precipice beyond the trees. They were heading straight toward the river and the walking bridge that arched across it. "Jase? That bridge won't support us." Stopping didn't seem like an option right now. "Do I turn upstream? You don't want me to turn around and play chicken with him, do you?" As the trees thinned near the water, she saw nothing but a drop-off and the water tumbling over the edge of the cliff into blue sky. They were running out of road. "Jase?"

"Hang a right." He fired off two more shots.

"Are you kidding me?" Cliff? Waterfall? Blue sky?

"The river runs pretty deep this time of year." He lurched behind her, squeezing the sentence through gritted teeth at her ear. "It runs a good distance before dropping off into the canyon."

"But—"

"Rule one!" A second man had joined the chase. Jason traded shots with him, too.

"Do whatever you say."

"We're going to be okay, Sam." He slapped his hand over hers, opening the throttle up as high as it would go. "Gun it!"

"Oh, I am so moving to sea level." Samantha tightened her grip and veered off the road, screaming every inch of the way as the edge of the cliff raced up to them. At the very last second Jason's arms cinched around her and he jerked her off the back of the vehicle. They hit the ground hard and rolled as the snowmobile sailed off over the waterfall ahead of them. A split second later, she tumbled over the edge of the embankment, locked in Jason's arms.

What had she thought earlier about sprouting wings and flying? She got a glimpse of the snowmobile crashing into the rocks on the opposite bank of the river. Flames erupted, and black smoke billowed up, filling the air with the pungent stench of burning fuel.

But a glimpse was all she got. She had one moment to notice the stink and heat of the fire in the air, and bruises and scrapes dotting her skin.

And then she was plunging into the frigid water.

Shock knocked the breath right out of her and she swallowed a mouthful of water. The current tossed her forward even as she sank until her feet hit the gritty bottom. She grabbed for her glasses and clutched them to her face, even though there was little to see.

Before she could orient herself, she felt a jerk on her shoulders. A long, strong arm reached down through the water for her. Once she understood that Jason had grabbed the strap of her backpack, she kicked toward the surface, helping them both swim upward until their heads cleared the surface. She coughed her aching lungs clear and tread water to keep her head above water while the current quickly swept them downstream. Jason left his arm threaded through the straps of her pack, linking them together. He coughed a few times, too. Water dribbled from his beard stubble, and his skin was pale, probably like her own.

"Keep moving so we have some chance of staying warm." The din of hornets in pursuit faded. They left the burning heap and angry, greedy men behind them as they bobbed along down the river. "Stay afloat. Let the current take us. Stealing the snowmobile was a good idea. No way can they catch up to us now. We'll be in civilization before they do."

Samantha circled her arms in front of her and kicked from time to time, despite the cold seeping into every pore of her body. "What about the next waterfall?"

"We'll be on dry land before we get there. Trust me."

"Always."

She didn't know how many yards, maybe even a mile or more, they'd floated, slowly descending the mountain as the river raced toward the valley before Jason paddled toward the shore and her feet touched solid land again. True to his word, they'd left the river before faced with the next obstacle of a taller, more powerful waterfall and its potentially deadly drop. But her teeth were chattering, and he was shivering as they crawled up the bank to more even ground and rolled over onto their backs, blinking up at the clear, sunny sky.

She went willingly when he turned her into his arms after a little bit and hugged her tightly against his chest. He pressed a kiss to the crown of her head and she nestled close, trading comfort as well as the last vestiges of body heat. "Bet you never thought in a million years you'd do something like that."

"It wasn't exactly on my bucket list."

She smiled at the soft rumble of laughter vibrating through his chest. If she wasn't so exhausted, she'd join him. When he went still beneath her cheek, she had the vague notion of dozing off with him for a few moments.

No, wait. Dozing was bad. Falling asleep might mean hypothermia. They needed to get up and get moving. Pushing against the ground and his chest, Samantha sat up. When she saw Jason's eyes were closed, a frisson of concern sparked a different sort of heat inside her. "Jase? Wake up." She gently tapped at his cheek, urging him back to consciousness. "What do we do now, mountain man?"

His dark lashes fluttered against his cheek and one granite-colored eye popped open. "Mountain man? I thought we weren't doing nicknames, Princess."

Silly with relief to hear him joking, she leaned down and kissed him, carefully avoiding the swollen cut on his bottom lip. He, however, seemed less concerned about any pain she might be causing him because he palmed the back of her head and held her lips against his as he deepened the kiss, sliding his tongue alongside hers until the cooler temperature of his skin registered and she pulled away. "All right. I deserve that one. I've followed the rest of your rules. Tell me what to do or I'll think you don't care about me anymore."

"I care." He answered the teasing challenge by sitting up, the lines beside his eyes deepening with the seriousness of his tone. "About getting you home. About doing right by you."

"You haven't failed me yet," she assured him, wondering if he'd been this hard on himself before losing his girlfriend when he'd been in the Corps. "You won't. Tell me what to do."

"Empty the water out of our boots. Wring our socks dry as best we can." After spending a few minutes doing just that, he pulled her to her feet. "And then we walk. As far and as fast as we can. If we're lucky, Buck will think we're dead. His men will search the crash and the river. Look." He pointed to the green grass and tiny shoots of wildflowers and succulents pushing up through the dirt. "No more snow. Unless they get a visual on us, they won't find any tracks. If we're really lucky, we'll run into a forest ranger or somebody out hiking or camping. Keep your head covered. If you lose sensation in your toes or fingers, let me know. But moving should help us warm up."

Jason forged ahead along the top of the riverbank, his fingers staying near his gun. His gaze swiveled from side to side, continuously looking for any sign of Buck or his men, even though she saw nothing but the scenery and heard nothing but the wind through the trees and the river powering its way down the mountain beside them.

That scenery included keeping her eye on the man ahead of her. Despite the afternoon sun rising high overhead, slowly drying the outer layers of their clothes to the extent that she shed her coat and he tied his jacket around his waist to let the warming air dry the sweaters and T-shirts they wore underneath, Jason's pace was slowing. And where the ground was uneven, he stumbled, catching himself with a muttered curse. His injuries and constantly being on alert were taking a toll on him. When he tripped again, Samantha looked down at the ground and uttered a choice word herself.

"Jason?" She pointed to the drops of blood on the ground. "You're leaving a trail."

When he turned, she saw a crimson blot about the size of her fist staining the front of his sweater, just above his waist. "So that second guy may have clipped me with one of those shots. The cold water slowed the bleeding for a while. But now that we're warming up—"

"Damn you and your stubborn Marine-headedness." She marched up to him and pushed to the nearest rock to sit him down.

"Marine-headedness? Is that a thing?" He looked down at her, watching her slide his pack off his shoulders and pull out the first aid kit. The fact that he was making light of his newest injury probably meant he was hurt worse than he was letting on.

"Be honest with me," she ordered, dumping the wet contents of the kit and a little stream of water in her lap. She needed something dry to stanch the bleeding. She untied her coat from her waist, pulled out her Swiss Army knife and started ripping it apart at the seams. "How badly are you hurt?"

"It may have nicked a rib and torn some muscle, but this one went through."

He lifted his sweater and T-shirt when she moved around him, inspecting the neat, finger-sized hole in the lower-left part of his back. She cleaned the wounds and folded the shreds of her coat lining into two small packets. She had him hold one over the wider exit wound in the front of his flank while she tied them both into place with the belt from her coat. "Stop getting hurt."

"Not my intention, honey. But better me than you."

"No. Not better. I need you alive. I need *you*."

Before she could analyze all the ways she meant that last confession, she dug into his pack for anything else she could secure the bandages with. "Your phone!" Her fingers closed around his cell phone and she pulled it out. "Do you think we have cell service yet? I'm calling 9-1-1. Or my father. He'll mobilize the National Guard if we need it." She was frustrated to see the black screen that refused to light up. Water dripped from the battery casing when she opened it up, as well. "It's as wet as we are. Unless we can dry out the components, it won't work."

"I've still got one of their radios."

She used nearly every inch of tape in the kit to secure the bandages around his waist before she pulled his T-shirt and sweater back down to cover the makeshift bandage. "The river might have ruined it, too. The battery pack won't make a good connection."

"Don't worry. You'll fix it." After repacking what was left of their things into one pack, she looped it over her shoulders and helped him up. He draped his arm around her shoulders, partly for warmth, partly for support. Samantha wound her arm around his waist, sharing whatever strength she had. He pressed a kiss to her temple and started walking, leaning on her a little as he limped along beside her. "If you can fix me, Sam, you can fix anything."

Why didn't she think he was talking about bullet holes?

Chapter Eleven

Never in a million years would Jason have guessed that a nearsighted heiress, with clothes that didn't fit, no filter on her thoughts and a seriously sweet set of lips, would be helping him hike the gravel road from the foot of the Grand Teton past one of the elk preserves outside Moose, Wyoming. He was the search and rescue expert. He was the tough-as-nails Marine, trained to do or die to complete his mission.

Sam Eddington had more backbone than any man or woman he'd served with. She was braver than any officer he'd served under. And she was more resourceful than anyone he knew, period. He'd sorely underestimated the challenge of this mission. Even more, he'd underestimated the woman he'd been sent to rescue.

Sam was funny, compassionate, frustrating, surprising, strong and sexy in ways he wasn't sure she fully comprehended. But Jason did. He wasn't sure exactly how he was going to walk out of her life and return to his solitary ways once he'd safely handed her over to her father. He was damn sure he wasn't going to forget their time together. Whether facing down danger or facing his past, she hadn't once retreated. But it wasn't like they had anything in common beyond having a band of mercenaries hunting them across the mountain. He was hardly the stuff relationships were made of, and he wasn't likely to fit in at the latest Eddington soiree or Midas Group board meeting. And he still wasn't certain he could handle being with someone if there was the possibility he could lose her again.

Not for the first time during these past days, he wondered if he'd finally achieved the redemption he'd sought for losing so much in Kilkut. While he tried not to lean too heavily on her shoulders as his wounds left his balance and stamina a little iffy, he wondered if redemption was enough. Or if there was an outside chance that his life could be about something more.

He smiled down at the top of Sam's head as she broke that silence that had lasted for oh, say, the last fifty yards. "You're certain you recognized the man on the snowmobile?"

"I'm certain. Orin Murphy. He's a friend of Richard Cordes Jr.'s. His cousin, I believe."

Sam nodded. "I heard Buck call him 'cuz' over the radio when he was chasing us. Do you think Buck is the same guy you called Junior? Buck wasn't in the van or on the mountain when I was first taken to that cabin. He could have been at the bar with you and Dad, and then he could have joined the group later once we went on the run."

"Orin's and Junior's dads were both part of that homegrown militia that kidnapped your mother." Jason squeezed her shoulder, apologizing for the sad and frightening memories this discussion she kept coming back to must trigger for her. But she wasn't the only one who needed to understand why this had happened. "This isn't about the money at all. It's about revenge."

"It's probably about the money for some of them. I'm guessing Junior hired whatever help family loyalty couldn't buy. Five million dollars can be pretty persuasive."

"Your father would never hire anyone he knew was related to Cordes. So how did he get a man inside your circle of friends and family?"

"What if Dad didn't know? Dante Pellegrino could organize something like a kidnapping and mercenaries. And Kyle would probably do it for the money. Or to get rid of me so he could have Taylor and still be a part of the Midas Group. Could Taylor have dated one of Cordes's friends or met him in college?"

"It's all speculation until the FBI launches an investigation and we can get answers." Jason dutifully put his thumb up when he heard the vehicle approaching from behind them. But the minivan filled with tourists was smart enough not to pick up hitchhikers in this remote stretch of wilderness in the southeastern edge of the national park. It skirted into the far lane and drove on past.

Sam's weary sigh echoed his own. "How much

farther do we have to go before we reach a farmhouse or some kind of road-stop business?"

"Don't think about it. Just keep walking."

"That's rule number six, I think. A raised fist means stop. Do what I say. Don't get wet. Don't fall off the mountain—"

"Enough. Am I really that much of a bossy jerk?"

"Yes. Well, the bossy part."

When he laughed, he winced and grabbed his side, forcing them to stop as pain radiated through him. Sam tried to get him to rest on the shoulder of the road, but Jason shook his head, breathing through the pain. At the rate his reserves of energy were failing him, he might not get up again if he sat down. Besides, this terrain was far too flat and open for him to feel he could protect her here. "We need to keep moving. Find shelter if we can't get help."

"We'll get help," she insisted, wrapping her arm around his waist and taking more of his weight as they continued at a slower pace.

And, as usual, she talked. "I've only met Richard Cordes Jr. one time. At his father's execution. Dad wouldn't let me go to the trial. How does a virtual stranger plan a kidnapping? How did he know where I'd be that night? How did his men know when I'd be alone? When they could abduct me? They were waiting for me at the lodge. It wasn't any spur-of-the-moment thing."

"An inside job."

"You think somebody I know…somebody I trusted…

is working with Buck? Do you think my father knows we have a traitor in our lives? Is he safe?"

"I don't know. All the more reason to get you back to Jackson. I want to know who set you up."

"Get in line behind me." She startled when a car honked at them, warning them to move onto the shoulder of the road before racing around them and kicking up a cloud of dust and stinging gravel they had to shield their eyes against. He was guessing the word she uttered wasn't welcome at Eddington parties, either. "Even if they don't want to pick up strangers who look as raggedy as we do, you'd think someone would at least stop and call the authorities for us."

"Might be the gun I'm wearing."

"Or the blood." He hated that he should be any part of the worry that puckered that little frown above her glasses. "Shoulder, stomach, back, thigh. You're pretty scary looking right now."

No doubt. "Want to split up? You're more likely to flag down someone to help on your own."

"You never left me. I'm not leaving you."

"I doubt these guys will try anything this close to civilization. They don't know we don't have a working cell phone and haven't called for help. If they're smart, they've already packed their gear and are heading north across the border as fast as they can get there before we sic the authorities on them and round up all the dead bodies."

"What if they're not smart? Buck or Richard Jr., or whatever he wants to call himself, seemed adamant about slicing and dicing me and serving me up on a platter to my dad. I'd feel better if we weren't out in the open like this." Good. Some of his survival skills were rubbing off on her.

"Want to try the radio again?"

"There's nothing else in this pack to cannibalize that will make it work."

As the dust from the last car settled, Jason noticed a second plume of dust kicking up behind a speeding vehicle. "Pickup truck at twelve o'clock. We'll try again."

"Hey! We need help!" Sam waved at the approaching black truck. It was an older model, but well taken care of by the sound of the engine. "Is he slowing down? He is." The truck flashed its lights at them and Sam waved. "He is!"

The pickup pulled off onto the opposite shoulder of the road. He averted his face as momentum carried the moving cloud of dust around the truck, obscuring his view of the driver. But as soon as it skidded to a stop, Sam was moving. Jason tightened his hold on her when she would have run forward to meet the man opening the grubby black door. "Let's see who we're dealing with before… Sam?"

"I know him." She broke free and ran across the road. "Brandon? Brandon!"

Jason recognized the lanky bodyguard who'd been ambushed the night Sam had been taken. Looked like he was wearing the same suit he had that night at the bar, only now his shirt collar was open, his tie was gone and the dark-haired man needed a shave.

"Samantha?" Metz climbed down from the running board and checked both ways for traffic before hurrying across the road to meet her. "I haven't been able to sleep for three days. I've felt so guilty. I've been looking everywhere for you."

"Thank God it's you." When the tall man bent slightly, Sam launched herself into his arms.

Even in his weakened state, Jason's instincts buzzed on high alert. This was wrong. Metz being here was wrong. Or maybe he was just having an irrationally possessive reaction to another man scooping Sam up and hugging her like that.

Pressing his fingers to the leaking bandage at his waist, Jason limped across the road to face Metz over the top of Sam's head. "Pellegrino and Mr. Eddington have run out of ideas to retrieve Sam beyond randomly driving around Wyoming?"

"Not random." Metz ended the hug but kept his arm around Sam's shoulders. "I knew which direction those men had taken her. Walter called in the FBI, despite the threats on that video, as soon as we got word that your man had crashed his helicopter and you two were stranded in the mountains."

"That man was Marty Flynn. His death was no accident. He gave his life trying to help us."

"I didn't mean to imply that he'd screwed up." The younger man raised his hands in apologetic surrender, releasing Sam long enough for Jason to pull her back to his side. "I'm sorry about your friend."

"You got a cell phone?" Jason prompted.

"Jason's hurt," Sam said. "He's been shot. Twice. Call an ambulance."

"Of course." Metz smiled down at Sam before reaching inside his jacket to pull out his cell.

Jason shook his head. "Call Walter first."

"Sure. You look like you're hurt pretty bad. Let's get you inside and off your feet." Avoiding Metz's offer to help, Jason leaned on Sam and walked around to the passenger side of the pickup. By the time he'd climbed onto the cracked white vinyl of the bench seat, Metz was standing there with a bottle of water. "Drink. If you've lost as much blood as I think you have, you need to replenish your fluids."

Jason took the water and thanked him for that, at least. "Make the call."

"May I talk to Dad?" Sam asked.

"Let me explain the good news to him, see how he wants me to handle this." He punched in a number and put the phone to his ear. "In the meantime, there's a blanket in the back of the truck. We don't want your friend here going into shock."

"Right."

As Metz's call went through, Jason turned his gaze to the rearview mirror and watched Sam lower the tailgate and climb into the back of the truck. He'd promised to get her back to her father, not to one of the family's bodyguards. His need to protect her hadn't diminished. Not by a long shot. But she didn't need to be married off to ensure her future. She didn't need to settle for a loser like Kyle Grazer. She could damn well take care of herself. The confidence that had been missing from their first meeting now radiated through every determined step and sharp-eyed glance.

It was those big green eyes meeting his gaze in the mirror through the back window that warned him a split second too late that his instincts had been right.

Sam scrambled over the side of the truck, carrying a black stocking mask in her hand. "There's a black camo uniform in a bag—"

"I know." She followed his gaze across the bench seat to see Metz at the driver's side door, pointing a gun right at him. "I found your inside man."

SAMANTHA GLARED THROUGH the windshield of the truck at the dark-haired psychopath who'd made it his life's work to punish her father for the death of his father.

Richard Cordes Jr. seemed to have an innate instinct as to what caused people the most pain. Watching him strike another blow to Jason's broken rib and open wound when the man she loved was already kneeling in the dirt with his hands bound in front of him cut through her as deeply as the length of Jason's knife plunging through her heart. Brandon had thrown that knife into the ditch along with the two guns they'd carried, leaving Jason completely unarmed before he forced him to drink the water from the bottle he'd given them—water which must have been laced with the same sedative she'd been injected with. At least she hoped that's why her savior had passed out on the long, bumpy ride into the

Wind River Mountains on the other side of Jackson Hole. She couldn't bear to think that Jason might be dying because of the wounds Junior and his men had inflicted on him each time they'd gotten close to recapturing her.

Since her dad had bought the land once illegally claimed by Junior's father, Richard Cordes II—he preferred the tougher-sounding nickname Buck to the diminutive *Junior* he apparently had grown up with—had secured a ramshackle house on what she assumed was an abandoned farm, based on the weedy fields and empty pastures they'd passed before the sun had set. She'd heard enough of his posturing through the open truck window to know he thought of this place as his new compound. He'd build an empire bigger and stronger than his father and aunts had owned, and no one, not even a *rich old bastard like Walter Eddington* or the US government, would be able to take it from him.

She recognized Orin Murphy from the mountain, too. Although his black eye and the tender way he carried himself indicated he was still feeling the effects of his run-in with Jason and a tree branch, he, like three other men in black camo gear, stood in a circle around Jason. Apparently, there was no electricity running at this remote location, either, because the men had all parked their trucks in a semicircle around Jason and the side of the house, spotlighting Junior—she refused to do him the honor of calling him Buck—while he rattled off some wild manifesto about the Second Amendment, injustices, and his vow to honor his father's legacy and avenge his death by the man who'd stolen that legacy—her father.

Brandon had parked his truck in the semicircle, too. He was one of these nut jobs with a skewed idea of right and wrong. His traitorous butt was so getting fired once she got back to her father. *If* she ever got back to him. Beyond that, she'd make sure there was jail time for each one of Junior's accomplices. They'd left three of Junior's men dead on the mountain, but they might be the lucky ones once she was done testifying about all she'd seen and heard and been subjected to, and the money and connections her father wielded made sure the very best lawyers in the country prosecuted them.

Of course, that kind of real justice depended on whether she survived this night. And even if she lived through it, she didn't think she'd survive if Jason didn't live through it, too.

Junior smacked his fist across Jason's face, knocking him onto his side on the ground.

"Stop it!" Sam yelled, distracting Junior from the torture.

But the young man with the pistol at his waist and the rifle hanging across his back merely looked at her through the windshield of the truck and laughed. "Aw. Does this upset you, rich girl? Seeing your big man bleedin' in the dirt? Just imagine how much fun I'm going to have doing the same thing to you."

"Damn it, Buck," Brandon complained, taking a step toward his cousin. "Quit playing games. You promised me a million dollars to bring Samantha to you. You already screwed up any chance at getting paid the ransom. Let's cut our losses. Finish them both off and at least let me turn her body back in to Eddington for a reward."

"A reward?" Junior turned his full attention on his cousin. "You think I want Eddington to have any kind of closure? Any kind of comfort?"

Oh, no. Brandon pulled back his jacket, bracing his hands on his hips, making sure Junior saw that he, too, carried a gun and knew how to use it. This was about to turn into a violent confrontation—some sort of Wild West shoot-out—and Jason would be caught in the crossfire. How could she get him out of there? How could she protect him?

Samantha's hands chafed against the rope that bound them. Brandon had left her in the truck trussed up like prized prey at the wrists and ankles when he'd pulled a semiconscious Jason out and thrown him to the ground at Junior's feet. *"You promised ten thousand dollars to the man who brought you Hunt. Pay up."*

Ten thousand dollars. She nearly cried remembering that taunt. Jason's life was worth so much more than that. His heart, his spirit, his soul were priceless. He'd served his country. He'd sacrificed his friends, the woman he loved and even a little part of his sanity. He'd saved her.

She had to save him.

As she struggled to slide across the seat to reach

the locked door, Samantha's fingers brushed against the bulge in her front pocket and she froze.

Jason might be unarmed. But she wasn't.

"Bless you, Marty Flynn." She contorted her body to get her hands close enough to her pocket to slide her fingers inside. "You're going to save us, after all."

While Brandon stood his ground and Junior spewed more vitriol about her father and how her mother deserved to be taken from him all those years ago, Samantha opened Marty's Swiss Army knife and sawed at her bindings.

"You never even would have thought you could get money like that until I put the idea in your head," Junior bragged. "I'm the one who said you needed to become her friend, so she'd turn to you when the opportunity came. I'm the one who told you to capitalize on her boyfriend's infidelities."

"Eddington trusted me," Brandon argued. "I had a good thing going there. Hell, given enough time, I could have ingratiated myself with the family and married Samantha myself. I didn't need you to do anything for me. I let you take a swing at me to make that kidnapping look real. Fired a couple of shots at the van while your men sped away. I did what I did for the money, so you could have your revenge. You owe me."

"I owe no man," Junior spouted, possibly quoting something his father had once said. "I am what I am because of who I am. And no greedy bastard will ever take my pride, my land, my manhood from me."

Brandon reached for his gun. "Shut up, already."

But Junior was faster. Samantha jerked, dropping the knife, catching it between her thighs when the gun went off and Brandon crumpled to the ground beside Jason.

She watched Jason's big form roll away from the dead man. Not only was he still alive, but he roused the strength to push himself up to a sitting position. In the light from the headlamps, she could see one of his handsome eyes had swollen shut, and the circle of blood on the front of his sweater had spread to cover nearly half his torso. He was bleeding badly. He needed her help.

Moving the knife back to her fingers again, she sawed away at the rope.

"All I wanted was Samantha Eddington at my mercy." Thank goodness Junior was more interested in hearing himself talk than in paying attention to her now. "I wanted to send pictures to her father and watch Walter's grief when he discovered what was left of her body. I had to stage it as a kidnapping, so I could convince these idiots to help me. Promised them each a ton of money. I'd have taken it, too. Enjoyed every penny. It's the least Eddington owes my family."

Jason's voice was low, yet surprisingly strong. "How'd you ensure their loyalty once they knew the ransom wasn't coming?"

"I lied. Just like I lied at Kitty's Bar in Moose that night you got mixed up in this. Set up my own alibi while my cousins and friends took Samantha. Right from under Eddington's nose. I've got no quarrel with you, Jase. But you keep getting in the way of what I want."

The ropes scraped across her skin as she broke free. "I will protect Sam until my dying breath."

"That's what I figured." Junior raised his gun. Samantha jammed the pocketknife's blade into the ignition and turned it.

Junior looked her way, startled to hear the engine roaring to life.

But that wasn't half as startled as he looked when she stomped on the accelerator with both feet and plowed into him.

The wall of the house caved in as she pinned him against the rotted siding.

Bits of roofing and a rusted gutter rained down on the hood of the truck. Tears burned down her cheeks and she swiped them away, unsure why she was crying now when she'd already been through so much.

But as she cleared her vision and shifted the truck into Park, she realized she'd made a tactical error. Junior was trapped, but he wasn't dead. And despite the way his body sagged between the truck and the house, she hadn't caught his arm in the crash. The arm that still held the gun.

With the slow deliberation of a madman, he dragged the gun up onto the hood of the truck and aimed it through the windshield. "You just have to die," he slurred as blood appeared in his mouth.

Samantha dived for the seat as the windshield shattered.

There was a second explosion. Two gunshots.

She tried to shift into Reverse from the awkward position, not wanting to raise her head above the dashboard while he kept firing.

But after two shots, she heard no more.

She heard only Jason's deep voice, ragged with pain. "It's okay, Sam. You can come out. You're safe."

She slowly sat up, averting her gaze from the gruesome sight of Richard Cordes's dead body slumped over the hood of the truck. She looked out the side window to see Jason on his knees, the barrel of the gun he held still steaming in his hands.

A closer look revealed that Brandon's holster was empty. Jason had taken the gun off the slain bodyguard and saved her, even as she'd saved him.

She looked beyond him as he swung the gun around to see Orin Murphy toss his weapons on the ground. He collapsed on the running board of his truck, cradling his middle as if the bones inside were cracked or broken. The other three men in black camo followed suit, dropping their weapons and kneeling with their fingers laced above their heads as Jason instructed.

Samantha wasted no more time. She retrieved Marty's knife from the floorboard and cut her ankles free. Then she was out of the truck and hurrying to Jason's side.

"Jase? Are you all right? Please tell me you're going to be all right." She inspected his face, lifted his shirt to check his wound. She took the knife to the ropes at his wrists, freeing him the way he had once freed her. "Why aren't you saying anything?" she demanded, tossing the bindings aside.

"Because you're doing all the talking, woman." He caught a loose tendril of hair and rubbed it between his fingers and thumb. "If you're okay, I'll be okay."

"I'm okay. You're okay, too, right?" She nodded, knowing that was a lie. Her hair fell from his fingers and he collapsed to the ground. "Jase?"

She picked up the gun and pointed it at the men who'd surrendered their weapons. "You all know who I am?" They nodded, chiming in with a few hesitant *yeah*s and saying her name. "I'll pay a hundred grand to the first man who gives me a working cell phone and the keys to his truck."

All four men held out their phones.

Chapter Twelve

"I love him, Dad."

Samantha hugged her father in the hospital's second-floor waiting room outside the surgical ICU. There wasn't anything this fine hospital could do to make her feel better after the kidnapping and survival ordeal than a shower, clean clothes and a hug from her father could. The bright, sunny afternoon and news that Jason had come through his surgery without any unexpected complications didn't hurt, either.

Walter Eddington pulled back, capturing her face between his beefy hands and offering her a wry smile. "You know, you never once said that about Kyle."

Samantha was even feeling generous enough to share a smile with her stepmother and Taylor, who'd brought the change of clothes to the Jackson hospital and had waited with her until the surgeon had come out to give her a report on Jason's condition. "I don't mention what's-his-face anymore. It's one of the rules Jase and I agreed on."

He caressed the silver locket and chain she'd returned to him, a little worse for wear after a long dip in a cold river, and slipped it into his pocket. "Captain Hunt makes you happy?"

"I think he will, Dad." If she could convince Jason of that.

"That's all I need to know. And we'll never mention what's-his-face again. It'll be like he never existed."

"I can live with that rule," Taylor agreed, turning a hopeful smile to her older sister. "I'm sorry for what I did. He said that he loved me. I don't know how I can ever make it up to you—or get over how stupid I feel for believing him."

Understanding exactly how her sister felt, Samantha reached out to hug her, too. "What's-his-face always seemed to know what to say. He just never learned how to listen. You and I will work on our relationship. We'll be okay."

Walter shook his head. "Looking back to the night you were taken, the way he was on his phone so much—I thought he might be involved in the kidnapping." Samantha grinned at the choice word he uttered. "With everything going on, he was more worried about himself. All those calls to his mother, playing the sympathy card of losing you to get back into his family's good graces."

Joyce slipped her arm through Walter's. Even her chemically peeled expression looked apologetic. "I for one am glad he moved back to New England. He wasn't hardy enough to thrive out West. To think his father didn't share that he'd cut Kyle, er, that man we can't mention, off from his trust fund and any future with the family business until he straightened up his act and stopped sleeping with his investors' wives and daughters. No wonder he was so desperate to marry into the family. You'd think that man had some kind of sexual illness."

Walter squeezed her hand where it rested on his arm. "I think that illness is called being a self-centered jackass."

Tipping her face to her father, her stepmother actually blushed. "I think you're right, dear." She raised her right hand and turned to Samantha and Taylor. "From now on, I leave my daughters' matchmaking…to my daughters. I'm just glad we're all together again, and we're all safe."

"I second that." Walter dipped his head to kiss her cheek. Samantha approved.

"Sam!"

She smiled. Finally. There was that voice. Bossy and deep, expecting answers and demanding action.

Jason shouted her name again from his room. Samantha stood there, her eyes tearing up with the emotional relief of all her fears and concern.

"Sam!"

Her sister giggled as her stepmother slipped her a tissue and her father nudged her toward his room. "You'd better go."

"Now stay put," a voice warned. A nurse brushed past her, mumbling something about hardheaded men as Samantha entered the recovery room. "Thank goodness you're here. Talk some sense into him."

She found Jason swinging one leg off the bed, trying to untangle himself from the monitor cords and IV attached to his hand. "What are you doing?" She rushed to his side, helping him settle back against the pillows. She adjusted his blue-and-white gown and pulled the covers up around his lap. "You're supposed to be resting."

When she checked his IV and the monitor clipped to his finger, he turned his hand to grab hold of hers. "I didn't have eyes on you. And that stupid nurse wouldn't answer any questions about you because I'm not family. Are you all right? Were you admitted to the hospital? What happened to Orin Murphy and the others at the compound?"

She perched on the side of the bed, appreciating the rugged lines of his cheeks and jaw that had been shaved so the doctors could address some of his injuries. Although she did miss the wiry scruff of dark stubble that had tickled her lips and palms.

"I'm okay," she assured him, cradling his hand between both of hers. "A doctor checked me out for exposure, hypothermia. They drew blood to see if there's any residue from the drug they used on me in my system—there's not. And they doctored a few scrapes and contusions. You're the one who was in surgery for three hours. Two broken ribs, a nick in your kidney, debriding wounds, stitches and staples— it's a wonder you're still alive and causing so much trouble."

"Don't joke about this. I know I was in and out of consciousness. Cordes didn't hurt you? You're really okay?"

"I'm really okay." Maybe if she changed the subject, he'd relax, and ease the convulsing squeeze of his hand around her fingers. "Dad's here. He's having a long conversation with Mr. Pellegrino about his hiring practices."

"My conversation with Pellegrino would be short and sweet. I don't know if he's ignorant or incompetent, but he can't be in charge of your security anymore."

She could feel him calming down enough to risk teasing him. "Maybe we'd better let Dad oversee diplomacy. You can be in charge of keeping me safe."

"You're offering me a job as a bodyguard?"

"I'm not offering you a job. I... What I want is... What I mean to say..." Since when did she get tongue-tied? Even when her words made no sense, she'd never had a problem getting them out.

"Hey." Jason pulled her hand onto his thigh, capturing her against the warmth of the blanket and the man underneath. "Come on. Seventy-two hours on that mountain with you, and I never once had to wonder what you were thinking. Talk to me."

Samantha nodded, heartened by his indulgent smile. Strengthened by the knowledge that he always had, and always would, listen to the truth behind what she had to say. She scooted closer. "Thank you for accepting me for who I am, and how I am. Quirks and baggage and all."

"Not a problem. You accepted me, and I will put my baggage up against yours any day."

"Agreed." Her fingers danced against the cotton blanket. She hadn't expected this to be so hard. Maybe it was hard because she suddenly realized his response was the most important thing in the world to her, right after learning he was still alive and would fully recover.

"What else, Sam?" He stilled her nervous fingers. His beautiful granite eyes locked on to hers, touching her with the same gentle strength of his hand. "I dumped everything on you. You can tell me anything."

"You really do listen to me." She reached up to touch his face. He smiled. Suddenly, this was easy. "Do you believe a person can fall in love in seventy-two hours? That you can know a person, inside and out, trust and respect that person, and lose your heart in that short a time?"

"Yes." He didn't hesitate to answer. He pulled her onto his lap and tucked her head beneath his chin, holding her close. Although he didn't protest any strain against his injuries, she held herself as still as possible and snuggled into his warmth and strength. "It happened to me. I love you, Sam. I didn't know I *could* love anymore. Sure as hell didn't think I was worthy of it. But you make me feel and want and I'm…better…when I'm with you. A better man. Better at saying what I think and admitting what I feel. I've been avoiding life and people and caring for a long time. But I don't want to anymore. I want to live and laugh and love and be with you. I'm probably still going to be a mess some days, but…" When he realized she was crying against his neck, he wiped away her tears. "I want to be a better man for you."

"You save people, Jason. You saved me. There isn't anything better than that."

"You saved *me*. In more ways than you'll ever know. You have more money than I'll make in my lifetime, but I don't want a penny of it. I want to live in the mountains—I don't think I could handle the city. I'm damaged, you're crazy smart or maybe just crazy, but I love that about you. I want to be your man. I want you to be my woman. If there's any way in hell you think this would work."

Samantha smiled then.

"I think…if we lay down a few ground rules… maybe different ones than mountain rules…" She stroked her fingers across his lips, finding an un-bruised place where she could press her mouth against his. "With your experience, my brains—and our love—I think we have a very good chance at making this work."

Epilogue

Seven months later

October in the Teton Mountains was a beautiful time of year. At the lower elevations, the trees were a riot of red, gold and orange leaves, while the evergreens higher up stood out in sharp contrast against the first layers of new snow.

Samantha cradled the steaming cup of coffee between her hands to warm them as she stood on the front porch of Jason's cabin—their cabin now—and surveyed the beautiful, rugged wilderness that reminded her so much of the man she loved. These mountains had once nearly killed her, but now she was beginning to think of them as her home.

As for any lingering fear or worries that she could be kidnapped again, Samantha tempered her new alertness to the people and places around her with a bone-deep trust that Jason Hunt would always have her back. He was more than enough security for her when they were alone like this. Even when she was at a Midas Group function surrounded by her father's new security team, she knew there was no one more focused on keeping her safe than Jason. And though their fears might stem from different causes, she took pride in knowing that she provided the emotional security Jason seemed to need, too.

She heard a whisper of sound as the door opened behind her. "I'm ready to head out." Jason had a deep, growly, sexy voice in the morning, and simply hearing it made her shiver with awareness.

Samantha set her mug on the railing and faced him, crossing the porch to check the zipper of his jacket and make sure he was wearing several layers of clothing. "Good morning to you, too. And goodbye, I guess. Got your gloves? Hat? The temperatures are starting to drop higher up the mountains."

"Who's the mountain guide and rescue expert here?" he teased, capturing her hands against his chest and smiling down at her. "What will you be doing while I'm rock climbing? Working on that eco-friendly waste disposal system you designed?"

"Uh-huh. Thanks for letting me experiment on your home."

"Hey, if I didn't know how good you are at tinkering with things and making them work, I wouldn't let you near the place."

"Liar. Rule one is to always be honest with each other."

"Okay. Truth is you can do whatever you want to my plumbing." The double entendre wasn't lost on Samantha. And when he dipped his head to steal a kiss, she wound her arms around his neck and let him take whatever he desired.

He'd loosened her hair from its ponytail and backed her against the post, before he finally pulled away, leaving the taste of him on her lips. "I'd better be going if I want to make it back in time to clean up for dinner with our parents."

Ignoring the frissons of passion still lingering from that kiss, Samantha turned the conversation to a more serious subject. "I know you need a little alone time before you tackle whatever's been on your mind these last few days. You do know you can talk to me about anything, right?"

"I know. The counselor says I'm continually improving. I'm doing better with groups of people. I'm able to talk more about some of my experiences when I first came home from overseas—like the day I went after the mailman because he gave my mom a package and I thought it was a bomb." Samantha reached for his hand. He might be making light of the frightening story he'd shared with her a month ago—how he'd scared his mother so badly that day that he'd moved out and hadn't looked back until reconnecting after Samantha's kidnapping. But she knew he was still dealing with some of the effects of his posttraumatic stress. He squeezed her fingers, silently thanking her for her support before releasing her. "I like the doctor's suggestion of adopting a pet, too. Maybe a big dog. One who'll go hiking with me."

"I'm just glad you're working on the relationship with your parents. How was Nolan's visit to the dermatologist?"

Fortunately, the illness Jason had been worried about was treatable. "They think they got all the melanoma cells off his face now. He'll have a scar that looks like a question mark. But that just makes him look cool."

She pulled a tube of sunscreen from the pocket of her jeans and stuck it in his backpack while he tugged his knit cap over his short, dark hair. "You should be watching your exposure to the sun at this altitude, too. Are you tackling the north face again? Or will you be working on clearing more of that trail up to Mule Deer Pass?"

"Neither. I'm just going for a day hike. Clearing my head."

"Why do you have to clear your head?" Samantha walked into his chest, wrapping her arms around his waist and snuggling beneath his chin. "Are you sure nothing's bothering you? Have I overstayed my welcome? Made the cabin too crowded for you?"

"No." He leaned back enough to capture her chin and tilt her lips up to his descending mouth. "Never."

Several minutes later they were back inside the cabin. The door was locked. Clothes were dropping as they made their way to the bedroom.

Jason skimmed his hands over her hips and rump and dragged her naked body up against the hard ridge that tented his shorts. Her breasts pillowed against the wall of his chest and her nipples caught in the wiry curls of his chest hair. They pearled into sweetly painful peaks that demanded the squeeze of his hand and the warm, moist stroke of his tongue. While he roused every cell, every nerve ending with the sweep of his big hands and greedy mouth, she caught his bottom lip between hers and nipped at the firm, masculine curve.

He moaned against her mouth. "You make me crazy when you do that."

"Crazy good?"

"Very good." He scooped her up and she hooked her legs around his waist, opening her heavy, weeping center to the fiery heat of his body.

They fell onto the bed together and they battled to find each other's most sensitive spots. The best angle for a kiss here. The lightest touch for a caress there. She was a tingling, quivering bundle of nerves, just waiting for the release she knew he could give her when he abandoned her for a moment, just long enough to shuck his shorts and roll a condom over his straining arousal.

"Are you sure you want to go hiking today?" she teased, her voice a husky, erotic plea.

"You're what I want today." When he returned to the bed, he flipped her onto her stomach, crawling behind her and entering her in one long, deep thrust. Samantha clutched a pillow in her fists, waiting helplessly for him to send her over the edge.

When he slipped his fingers beneath her, pressing against the nub of her arousal, she did just that, burying her face in the pillow and screaming his name as all sensibility shattered and she rode wave after wave of pleasure between his body and hand. Moments later, he groaned against the nape of her neck and poured himself out inside her.

It could have been seconds or minutes or even half a day that she lay there, sandwiched between Jason's body and hands, secure and replete in the weight and warmth of him spooned against her.

"I knew I'd like sex," she admitted on a satisfied whisper, rolling onto her back as he settled in beside her. "I just never knew it could be this good."

"That mouth." He kissed it soundly before climbing off the bed and crossing into the bathroom to wash up. "The sex is good because it's you and me. Everything is good because it's you and me."

Samantha put on her glasses and tucked the top sheet around her, sitting up to watch him pull on his shorts. The scars were still pink on his stomach, thigh and shoulder. But as far as Samantha was concerned, they were badges of honor, testaments to his bravery and commitment and just how lucky she was that he was a part of her life.

"If you're going to look at me like that, then I'm never going to get up that mountain."

"Like what?"

"Like you love me."

"I do."

"Here." He picked up his cargo pants from the floor and pulled a ring box from one of the pockets before sitting beside her on the edge of the bed. "This is why I've been a little distracted lately. I was going to do this tonight in front of Walter and Joyce and my parents. But I can't wait." He opened the box to show her a small, square-cut diamond in a white gold setting. "I love you, Sam. Will you marry me?"

The ring was as simple and beautiful and perfect as his proposal. "Yes."

* * * * *

Look for more stories of
thrilling romantic suspense
from USA TODAY *bestselling author Julie Miller*
coming in 2019

And don't miss these titles,
available now from Harlequin Intrigue:

APB: Baby
Kansas City Countdown
Necessary Action
Protection Detail
Military Grade Mistletoe
Kansas City Cop

SPECIAL EXCERPT FROM

When wealthy cattleman Callen Laramie is called back home to Coldwater, Texas, for a Christmas wedding, he has no idea just how much his attendance will matter to his family...and to the woman who's never been far from his thoughts— or his heart.

Read on for a sneak preview of
Lone Star Christmas
by USA TODAY *bestselling author*
Delores Fossen.

CHAPTER ONE

DEAD STUFFED THINGS just didn't scream Christmas wedding invitation for Callen Laramie. Even when the dead stuffed thing—an armadillo named Billy—was draped with gold tinsel, a bridal veil and was holding a bouquet of what appeared to be tiny poinsettias in his little armadillo hands.

Then again, when the bride-to-be, Rosy Muldoon, was a taxidermist, Callen supposed a photo like that hit the more normal range of possibilities for invitation choices.

Well, normal-ish anyway.

No one had ever accused Rosy of being conventional, and even though he hadn't seen her in close to fourteen years, Billy's bridal picture was proof that her nonnormalcy hadn't changed during that time.

Dragging in a long breath that Callen figured he might need, he opened the invitation. What was printed inside wasn't completely unexpected, not really, but he was glad he'd taken that breath. Like most invitations, it meant he'd have to do something, and doing something like this often meant trudging through the past.

Y'all are invited to the wedding of Buck McCall and Rosy Muldoon. Christmas Eve at Noon in the Lightning Bug Inn on Main Street, Coldwater, Texas. Reception to follow.

So, Buck had finally popped the question, and Rosy had accepted. Again, no surprise. Not on the surface anyway, since Buck had started "courting" Rosy several years after both of them had lost their spouses about a decade and a half ago.

But Callen still got a bad feeling about this.

The bad feeling went up a notch when he saw that the printed RSVP at the bottom had been lined through and the words handwritten there. "Please come. Buck needs to see you. Rosy."

Yes, this would require him to do something.

She'd underlined the *please* and the *needs*, and it was just as effective as a heavyweight's punch to Callen's gut. One that knocked him into a time machine and took him back eighteen years. To that time when he'd first laid eyes on Buck and then on Rosy shortly thereafter.

Oh man.

Callen had just turned fourteen, and the raw anger and bad memories had been eating holes in him. Sometimes, they still did. Buck had helped with that. Heck, maybe Rosy had, too, but the four mostly good years he'd spent with Buck couldn't erase the fourteen awful ones that came before them.

He dropped the invitation back on his desk and steeled himself up when he heard the woodpecker taps of high heels coming toward his office. Several taps later, his assistant, Havana Mayfield, stuck her head in the open doorway.

Today, her hair was pumpkin orange with streaks of golden brown, the color of a roasted turkey. Probably to coordinate with Thanksgiving, since it'd been just the day before.

Callen wasn't sure what coordination goal Havana had been going for with the lime-green pants and top or the lipstick-red stilettos, but as he had done with Rosy and just about everyone else from his past, he'd long since given up trying to figure out his assistant's life choices. Havana was an efficient workaholic, like him, which meant he overlooked her wardrobe, her biting sarcasm and the occasional judgmental observations about him—even if they weren't any of her business.

"Your two o'clock is here," Havana said, setting some contracts and more mail in his inbox. Then she promptly took the stack from his outbox. "George Niedermeyer," she added, and bobbled her eyebrows. "He brought his mother with him. She wants to tell you about her granddaughter, the lawyer."

Great.

Callen silently groaned. George was in his sixties and was looking for a good deal on some Angus. Which Callen could and would give him. George's mother, Myrtle, was nearing ninety, and despite her advanced age, she was someone Callen would classify as a woman with too much time on her hands. Myrtle would try to do some matchmaking with her lawyer granddaughter, gossip about things that Callen didn't want to hear and prolong what should be a half-hour meeting into an hour or more.

"Myrtle said you're better looking than a litter of fat spotted pups," Havana added, clearly enjoying this. "That's what you get for being a hotshot cattle broker with a pretty face." She poked her tongue against her cheek. "Women just can't resist you and want to spend time with you. The older ones want to fix you up with their offspring."

"You've had no trouble resisting," he pointed out—though he'd never made a play for her. And wouldn't. Havana and anyone else who worked for him was genderless as far as Callen was concerned.

"Because I know the depths of your cold, cold heart. Plus, you pay me too much to screw this up for sex with a hotshot cattle broker with a pretty face."

Callen didn't even waste a glare on that. The *pretty face* was questionable, but he was indeed a hotshot cattle broker. That wasn't ego. He had the bank account, the inventory and the willing buyers to prove it.

Head 'em up, move 'em out.

Callen had built Laramie Cattle on that motto. That and plenty of ninety-hour workweeks. And since his business wasn't broke, it didn't require fixing. Even if it would mean having to listen to Myrtle for the next hour.

"What the heck is that?" Havana asked, tipping her head to his desk.

Callen followed her gaze to the invitation. "Billy, the armadillo. Years ago, he was roadkill."

Every part of Havana's face went aghast. "Ewww."

He agreed, even though he would have gone for something more manly sounding, like maybe a grunt. "The bride's a taxidermist," he added. Along with being Buck's housekeeper and cook.

Still in the aghast mode, Havana shifted the files to her left arm so she could pick up the invitation and open it. He pushed away another greasy smear of those old memories while she read it.

"Buck McCall," Havana muttered when she'd finished.

She didn't ask who he was. No need. Havana had sent Buck Christmas gifts during the six years that she'd worked for Callen. Considering those were the only personal gifts he'd ever asked her to buy and send to anyone, she knew who Buck was. Or rather she knew that he was important to Callen.

Of course, that "important" label needed to be judged on a curve because Callen hadn't actually visited Buck or gone back to Coldwater since he'd hightailed it out of there on his eighteenth birthday. Now he was here in Dallas, nearly three hundred miles away, and sometimes it still didn't feel nearly far enough. There were times when the moon would have been too close.

Havana just kept on staring at him, maybe waiting for him to bare his soul or something. He wouldn't. No reason for it, either. Because she was smart and efficient, she had almost certainly done internet searches on Buck. There were plenty of articles about him being a foster father.

Correction: the hotshot of foster fathers.

It wouldn't have taken much for Havana to piece together that Buck had fostered not only Callen but his three brothers, as well. Hell, for that matter Havana could have pieced together the rest, too. The bad stuff that'd happened before Callen and his brothers had gotten to Buck's. Too much for him to stay, though his brothers had had no trouble putting down those proverbial roots in Coldwater.

"Christmas Eve, huh?" Havana questioned. "You've already got plans to go to that ski lodge in Aspen with a couple of your clients. Heck, you scheduled a business meeting for Christmas morning, one that you insisted I attend. Say, is Bah Humbug your middle name?"

"The meeting will finish in plenty of time for you to get in some skiing and spend your Christmas bonus," he grumbled. Then he rethought that. "Do you ski?"

She lifted her shoulder. "No, but there are worse things than sitting around a lodge during the holidays while the interest on my bonus accumulates in my investment account."

Yes, there were worse things. And Callen had some firsthand experience with that.

"Are you actually thinking about going back to Coldwater for this wedding?" Havana pressed.

"No." But he was sure thinking about the wedding itself and that note Rosy had added to the invitation.

Please.

That wasn't a good word to have repeating in his head.

Havana shrugged and dropped the invitation back on his desk. "Want me to send them a wedding gift? Maybe they've registered on the Taxidermists-R-Us site." Her tongue went in her cheek again.

Callen wasted another glare on her and shook his head. "I'll take care of it. I'll send them something."

She staggered back, pressed her folder-filled hand to her chest. "I think the earth just tilted on its axis. Or maybe that was hell freezing over." Havana paused, looked at him. "Is something wrong?" she came out and asked, her tone no longer drenched with sarcasm.

Callen dismissed it by motioning toward the door. "Tell the Niedermeyers that I need a few minutes. I have to do something first."

As expected, that caused Havana to raise an eyebrow again, and before she left, Callen didn't bother to tell her that her concern wasn't warranted. He could clear this up with a phone call and get back to work.

But who should he call?

Buck was out because if there was actually something wrong, then his former foster father would be at the center of it. That *Please come. Buck needs to see you* clued him into that.

He scrolled through his contacts, one by one. He no longer had close friends in Coldwater, but every now and then he ran into someone in his business circles who passed along some of that gossip he didn't want to hear. So the most obvious contacts were his brothers.

Kace, the oldest, was the town's sheriff. Callen dismissed talking to him because the last time they'd spoken—four or five years ago—Kace had tried to lecture Callen about cutting himself off from the family. Damn right, he'd cut himself off, and since he would continue to do that and hated lectures from big brothers, he went to the next one.

Judd. Another big brother who was only a year older than Callen. Judd had been a cop in Austin. Or maybe San Antonio. He was a deputy now in Coldwater, but not once had he ever bitched about Callen leaving the "fold." He kept Judd as a possibility for the call he needed to make and continued down the very short list to consider the rest of his choices.

Nico. The youngest brother, who Callen almost immediately discounted. He was on the rodeo circuit—a bull rider of all things—and was gone a lot. He might not have a clue if something was wrong.

Callen got to Rosy's name next. The only reason she was in his contacts was because Buck had wanted him to have her number in case there was an emergency. A *please* on a wedding invitation probably didn't qualify as one, but since he hated eating up time by waffling, Callen pressed her number. After a couple of rings, he got her voice mail.

"Knock knock," Rosy's perky voice greeted, and she giggled like a loon. "Who's there? Well, obviously not me, and since Billy can't answer the phone, ha ha, you gotta leave me a message. Talk sweet to me, and I'll talk sweet back." More giggling as if it were a fine joke.

Callen didn't leave a message because a) he wanted an answer now and b) he didn't want anyone interrupting his day by calling him back.

He scrolled back through the contacts and pressed Judd's number. Last he'd heard, Judd had moved into the cabin right next to Buck's house, so he would know what was going on.

"Yes, it came from a chicken's butt," Judd growled the moment he answered. "Now, get over it and pick it up."

In the background Callen thought he heard someone make an *ewww* sound eerily similar to the one Havana had made earlier. Since a chicken's butt didn't have anything to do with a phone call or wedding invitation, it made Callen think his brother wasn't talking to him.

"What the heck do you want?" Judd growled that, too, and this time Callen did believe he was on the receiving end of the question.

The bad grouchy attitude didn't bother Callen because he thought it might speed along the conversation. Maybe. Judd didn't like long personal chats, which explained why they rarely talked.

"Can somebody else gather the eggs?" a girl asked. Callen suspected it might be the same one who'd ewww'ed. Her voice was high-pitched and whiny. "These have poop on them."

"This is a working ranch," Judd barked. "There's

poop everywhere. If you've got a gripe with your chores, talk to Buck or Rosy."

"They're not here," the whiner whined.

"There's Shelby," Judd countered. "Tell her all about it and quit bellyaching to me."

Just like that, Callen got another ass-first knock back into the time machine. Shelby McCall. Buck's daughter. And the cause of nearly every lustful thought that Callen had had from age fifteen all the way through to age eighteen.

Plenty of ones afterward, too.

Forbidden fruit could do that to a teenager, and as Buck's daughter, Shelby had been as forbidden as it got. Callen remembered that Buck had had plenty of rules, but at the top of the list was one he gave to the boys he fostered. *Touch Shelby, and I'll castrate you.* It had been simple and extremely effective.

"Buck got a new batch of foster kids," Judd went on, and again, Callen thought that part of the conversation was meant for him. "I just finished a double shift, and I'm trying to get inside my house so I can sleep, but I keep getting bothered. What do you want?" he tacked onto that mini-rant.

"I got Buck and Rosy's wedding invitation," Callen threw out there.

"Yeah. Buck popped the question a couple of weeks ago, and they're throwing together this big wedding deal for Christmas Eve. They're inviting all the kids Buck has ever fostered. All of them," Judd emphasized. "So, no, you're not special and didn't

get singled out because you're a stinkin' rich prodi-
gal son. *All of them*," he repeated.

Judd sounded as pleased about that as Callen
would have been had he still been living there. He
had no idea why someone would want to take that
kind of step back into the past. It didn't matter that
Buck had been good to them. The only one who had
been. It was that being there brought back all the
stuff that'd happened before they'd made it to Buck.

"Is Buck okay?" Callen asked.

"Of course he is," Judd snapped. Then he paused.
"Why wouldn't he be? Just gather the blasted eggs!"
he added onto that after another whiny *ewww.* "Why
wouldn't Buck be okay?"

Callen didn't want to explain the punch-in-the-gut
feeling he'd gotten with Rosy's *Please come. Buck
needs to see you*, and it turned out that he didn't
have to explain it.

"Here's Shelby, thank God," Judd grumbled before Callen had to come up with anything. "She'll
answer any questions you have about the wedding.
It's Callen," he said to Shelby. "Just leave my phone
on the porch when you're done."

"No!" Callen couldn't say it fast enough. "That's
all right. I was just—"

"Callen," Shelby greeted.

Apparently, his lustful thoughts weren't a thing
of the past after all. Even though Shelby was definitely a woman now, she could still purr his name.

He got a flash image of her face. Okay, of her
body, too. All willowy and soft with that tumble of

blond hair and clear green eyes. And her mouth. Oh man. That mouth had always had his number.

"I didn't expect you to be at Judd's," he said, not actually fishing for information. But he was. He was also trying to fight back what appeared to be jealousy. It was something he didn't feel very often.

"Oh, I'm not. I was over here at Dad's, taking care of a few things while he's at an appointment. He got some new foster kids in, and when I heard the discussion about eggs, I came outside. That's when Judd handed me his phone and said I had to talk to you. You got the wedding invitation?" she asked.

"I did." He left it at that, hoping she'd fill in the blanks of the questions he wasn't sure how to ask.

"We couldn't change Rosy's mind about using that picture of Billy in the veil. Trust me, we tried."

Callen found himself smiling. A bad combination when mixed with arousal. Still, he could push it aside, and he did that by glancing around his office. He had every nonsexual thing he wanted here, and if he wanted sex, there were far less complicated ways than going after Shelby. Buck probably still owned at least one good castrating knife.

"I called Rosy, but she didn't answer," Callen explained.

"She's in town but should be back soon. She doesn't answer her phone if she's driving."

Callen couldn't decide if that was a good or bad thing on a personal level for him. If Rosy had answered, then he wouldn't be talking to Shelby right now. He wouldn't feel the need for a cold shower or an explanation.

"Rosy should be back any minute now. You want me to have her call you?" Shelby asked.

"No. I just wanted to tell them best wishes for the wedding. I'll send a gift and a card." And he'd write a personal note to Buck.

"You're not coming?" Shelby said.

Best to do this fast and efficient. "No. I have plans. Business plans. A trip. I'll be out of the state." And he cursed himself for having to justify himself to a woman who could lead to castration.

"Oh."

That was it. Two letters of the alphabet. One word. But it was practically drowning in emotion. Exactly what specific emotion, Callen didn't know, but that gut-punch feeling went at him again hard and fast.

"Shelby?" someone called out. It sounded like the whiny girl. "Never mind. Here comes Miss Rosy."

"I guess it's an important business trip?" Shelby continued, her voice a whisper now.

"Yes, longtime clients. I do this trip with them every year—"

"Callen, you need to come," Shelby interrupted. "Soon," she added. "It's bad news."

Don't miss
Lone Star Christmas *by Delores Fossen,*
available now wherever
HQN Books and ebooks are sold.

www.HQNBooks.com

INTRIGUE

Available October 16, 2018

#1815 RUGGED DEFENDER
Whitehorse, Montana: The Clementine Sisters • by B.J. Daniels
Cowboy Justin Calhoun is thrilled to see Chloe Clementine, the girl he has always loved, back in Whitehorse, Montana, for the holidays. Can he protect her from the secret Santa who is sending her dangerous gifts?

#1816 THE GIRL WHO WOULDN'T STAY DEAD
by Cassie Miles
When her wealthy ex-husband dies under suspicious circumstances, Emily Benton-Riggs inherits a home in Aspen and several artworks. Now someone is trying to kill her. Will Emily's longtime friend and lawyer, Connor Gallagher, be able to save her from the escalating threats to her life?

#1817 MURDER AND MISTLETOE
Crisis: Cattle Barge • by Barb Han
Rancher Dalton Butler and Detective Leanne West must work together to discover who murdered Leanne's niece and a girl from Dalton's past. As sparks fly between them, Dalton and Leanne will need to find the murderer before he or she chooses another victim...

#1818 DELTA FORCE DEFENDER
Red, White and Built: Pumped Up • by Carol Ericson
When impulsive Delta Force soldier Cam Sutton confronts brainy CIA translator Martha Drake about some mysterious emails, a sinister plot to contain the source of those emails endangers them both.

#1819 HIDE THE CHILD
by Janice Kay Johnson
Psychologist Trina Marr must protect a three-year-old child who is mute after witnessing the murder of her family. After the pair is almost killed, army ranger Gabriel Decker is sent to protect them, but a killer will do anything to stop the only witness to a heinous crime from telling the truth...

#1820 WYOMING COWBOY PROTECTION
Carsons & Delaneys • by Nicole Helm
Addie Foster takes a job as a housekeeper at Noah Carson's ranch to save her baby nephew. However, it's not long before the baby's mob-boss father finds her and begins threatening her. Can Noah protect the woman and child he has come to love?

YOU CAN FIND MORE INFORMATION ON UPCOMING HARLEQUIN® TITLES, FREE EXCERPTS AND MORE AT WWW.HARLEQUIN.COM.

HICNM1018

Get 4 FREE REWARDS!

We'll send you 2 FREE Books plus 2 FREE Mystery Gifts.

Harlequin® Intrigue books feature heroes and heroines that confront and survive danger while finding themselves irresistibly drawn to one another.

FREE Value Over $20

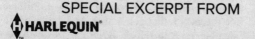
It all began with a kiss. At least that was the way Chloe
Clementine remembered it. A winter kiss, which is nothing like
a summer one. The cold, icy air around you. Puffs of white
breaths intermingling. Warm lips touching, tingling as they
meet for the very first time.

Chloe thought that kiss would be the last thing she
remembered before she died of old age. It was the kiss—and
the cowboy who'd kissed her—that she'd been dreaming about
when her phone rang. Being in Whitehorse had brought it all
back after all these years.

She groaned, wanting to keep sleeping so she could stay
in that cherished memory longer. Her phone rang again. She
swore that if it was one of her sisters calling this early…

"What?" she demanded into the phone without bothering
to see who was calling. She was so sure that it would be her
youngest sister, Annabelle, the morning person.

"Hello?" The voice was male and familiar. For just a
moment she thought she'd conjured up the cowboy from the
kiss. "It's Justin."

Justin? She sat straight up in bed. Thoughts zipped past at
a hundred miles an hour. How had he gotten her cell phone
number? Why was he calling? Was he in Whitehorse?

"Justin," she said, her voice sounding croaky from sleep. She cleared her throat. "I thought it was Annabelle calling. What's up?" She glanced at the clock. *What's up at seven forty-five in the morning?*

"I know it's early but I got your message."

Now she really was confused. "My message?" She had danced with his best friend at the Christmas dance recently, but she hadn't sent Justin a message.

"That you needed to see me? That it was urgent?"

She had no idea what he was talking about. Had her sister Annabelle done this? She couldn't imagine her sister Tessa Jane doing such a thing. But since her sisters had fallen in love they hadn't been themselves.

"I'm sorry, but I didn't send you a message. You're sure it was from me?"

"The person calling just told me that you were in trouble and needed my help. There was loud music in the background as if whoever it was might have called me from a bar."

He didn't think she'd drunk-dialed him, did he? "Sorry, but it wasn't me." She was more sorry than he knew. "And I can't imagine who would have called you on my behalf." Like the devil, she couldn't. It had to be her sister Annabelle.

"Well, I'm glad to hear that you aren't in trouble and urgently need my help," he said, not sounding like that at all.

She closed her eyes, now wishing she'd made something up. What was she thinking? She didn't need to improvise. She was in trouble, though nothing urgent exactly. At least for the moment.

Don't miss
Rugged Defender *by B.J. Daniels,*
available November 2018 wherever
Harlequin® Intrigue *books and ebooks are sold.*

www.Harlequin.com

HIEXP1018

Need an adrenaline rush from nail-biting tales
(and irresistible males)?

Check out **Harlequin Intrigue®**
and **Harlequin® Romantic Suspense** books!

New books available every month!

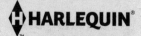

Love Harlequin romance?

DISCOVER.

Be the first to find out about promotions, news and exclusive content!

 Facebook.com/HarlequinBooks

 Twitter.com/HarlequinBooks

 Instagram.com/HarlequinBooks

 Pinterest.com/HarlequinBooks

ReaderService.com

EXPLORE.

Sign up for the Harlequin e-newsletter and download a free book from any series at **TryHarlequin.com.**

CONNECT.

Join our Harlequin community to share your thoughts and connect with other romance readers!
Facebook.com/groups/HarlequinConnection

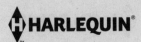

HARLEQUIN®

ROMANCE WHEN YOU NEED IT